THE BIG BOOK OF PUZZLE FUN

Over 500 Puzzles, Quizzes, and Brain Teasers

Hey, puzzle pals! Welcome to a great new volume of puzzling fun.

THE BIG BOOK OF PUZZLE FUN is for kids who like to think, for kids who like to have fun, and for kids who think they like to have fun. It has puzzles, games, jokes, magic tricks, quizzes, brain teasers, and all kinds of great stuff.

You'll see puzzles on animals, sports, school, vacation, travel, outer space, and almost anything you can imagine. There are mazes, crosswords, What's Wrong?, matching, and more. Mixed in with all this are some challenging Hidden Pictures puzzles, too. And be sure to keep an eye out for secret puzzles and mysterious cartoons.

Wow! That sure is a lot for one book. But before we get started, let's meet the kids who will help you through some of these different puzzles—The Puzzle Pals! Though we work together as a team, we each have our own special area. Our descriptions will give you an idea of the puzzles at which we each excel. And you'll get to know more about us as we go along.

So sharpen your pencils and let's get started!

Boyds Mills Press, Inc.
A Highlights Company
815 Church Street
Honesdale, Pennsylvania 18431
Printed in The United States of America
ISBN 1-56397-879-2

10 9 8 7 6 5 4 3 2 1

Puzzle Pals

Dotty
Until they're connected, she's never quite done.
Her magical dots are doorways to fun.

Missing Linc
Linc is always there, though not always seen. Just try to find him, and you'll know what we mean.

Roy G. Bivo
A creative wonder, with real style. Doing things artistic is what makes him smile.

Logical Lee
Lee has a logical mind. Give him some facts, the answer he'll find.

Rebus Rita
Rita sees pictures instead of words. She'll make you sound out the things you've heard.

Rambyte
This cranky computer has a personality all his own. He can show up anywhere, even when no one's home.

The Amazing Mazers
Left or right, which way should you go? The Mazers are the ones who'll know.

Holly & Molly
These girls are matching robotic sisters. When they don't agree, they blow their transistors.

Brainstorm Brian
Brian spends all of his time inventing. The things he creates are all "patent pending."

In no time, we'll be your best friends! After all, we're here to have fun with you. And to start off, let's head to the circus.

Down

6 12 20 1 25 21 15 2 4 13 26 16 7 28 10 14 5 22 19 7

At The Big Top

All the things pictured here can fit into the grid below. The pictures will tell you what words to write in which blocks. One page is for the Across answers, while the other page has the Down answers.

Across

For the answer, parade over to page 138.

Illustrated by R. Michael Palan

I WANT MY MAYPOLE!

How many differences can you find between these two pictures?

GIRAFFE MAZE

Just for fun, this little bug is trying to crawl from the giraffe's head down to the ground without stepping on any of the giraffe's spots. Can you find the path he will have to take?

Answer on page 138.

Nose and Toes Match-Up

Match the nose and toes of each of the eight animals shown below.

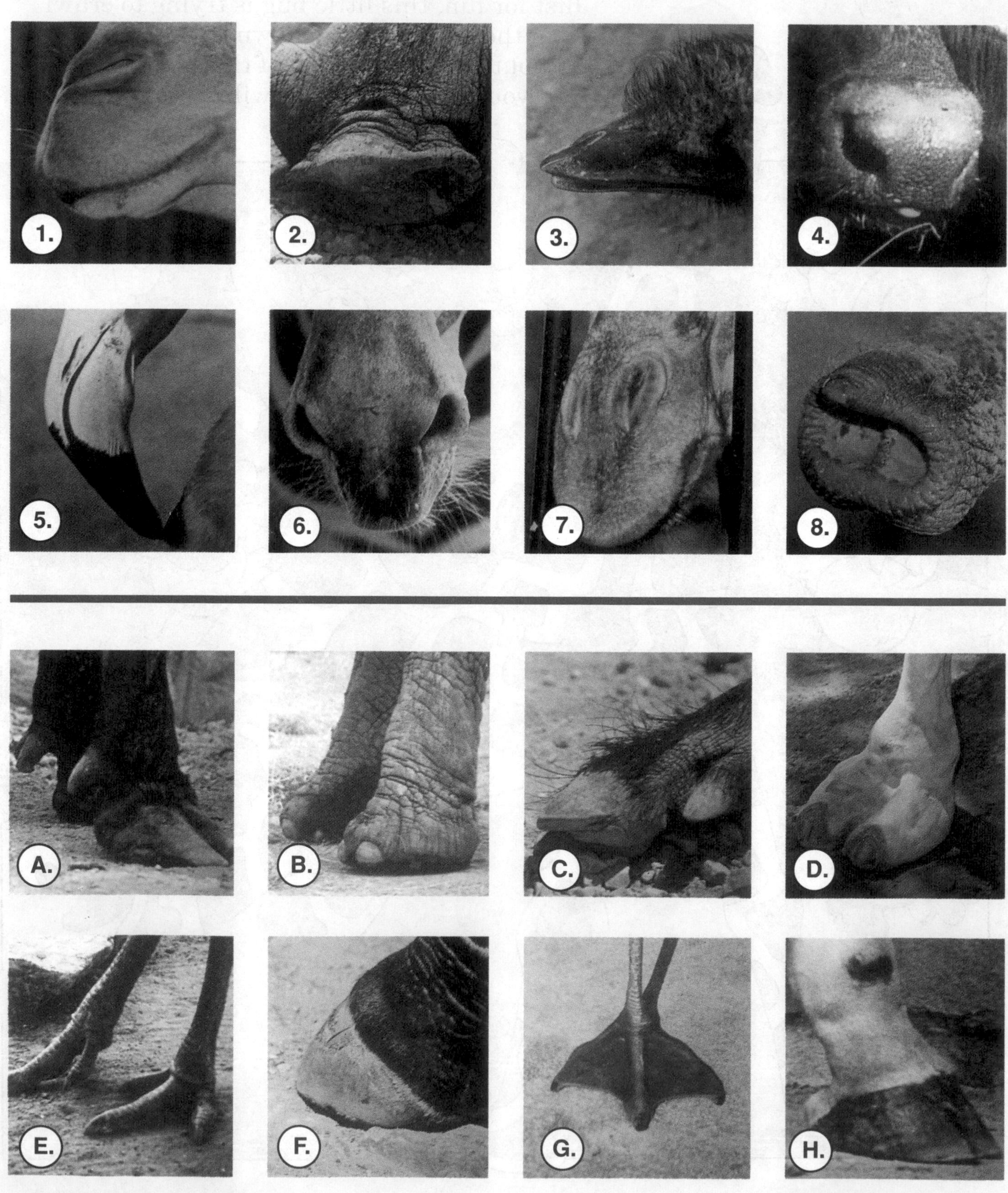

Answer on page 138.

ANIMAL CATCHPHRASES

Did you notice that there is a cat hiding in the title of this page? It's right at the beginning of CATchphrases. Each of the descriptions below can be defined by another word that has some animal hiding in it. Figure out as many words as you can and then circle the names of the animals.

1. Once in a while, every now and ______

____

2. A place for your cereal

____

3. A bird seen in the city

____

4. Cover for a sewer or heating duct

____

5. Person who plays behind home plate

____

6. The air we breathe

____

7. Huge fairy tale character

____

8. Vine fruit good for jam, jelly, and juice

____

9. Type of lion in "The Wizard of Oz"

____

10. 1,000,000

____

Answers on page 138.

JUNGLE JUMBLE

Stanley Livingston, that intrepid explorer, made a list of all the animals he saw while on safari. Unfortunately, he was so rushed, he crammed a few names together so that they came out as one name. Can you help Stanley figure out which two, three, or four animal names have been jumbled together?

HORSEALEOPARD
DOGIRAFFERRET
TIGERBIL
COWOLFOX
NARWHALEMULE
ELEPHANTELOPE
GORILLAMA
OKAPIGUANA

These names are cleared up on page 138.

SHADOWY SHAPES

Can you match these Oriental animals with their shadows?

Answers on page 138.

The Puzzle Pals have been sent to the National Zoo on matters of top security. To help them solve this vital riddle, read where each clue leads. Then, find the letter there and place it in the space above the number that matches the clue.

Where do spies sleep?

_ _ _ _ _ _ _ _ _ _ _
9 6 1 7 3 4 2 8 7 3 5

Clue No. 1
If you are right about this clue,
This animal will clap for you.

Clue No. 2
This clue will stand out fair and firm
When visiting the pachyderm.

Clue No. 3
No one here will shout or sing it.
For your next clue you'll have to "wing it."

Clue No. 4
Find this clue and don't get jumpy,
Though the ride could be bumpy.

Clue No. 5
The answers now are coming quick,
So find this clue and take a lick.

Clue No. 6
Take this letter from the horse,
The one that's wearing stripes, of course.

Clue No. 7
For this next clue—don't get annoyed
And wave "hi" to the anthropoid.

Clue No. 8
You will sure be helped a lotamus
If you find the hippopotamus.

Clue No. 9
You can find the next clue just like that,
But please don't pet this pussy cat!

Illustrated by OUT OF THE BLUE

Spy the answers on page 138.

Find the Friends

Howdy! Welcome to the Arizona Desert. Even in this land of sun, sand, stones, and saguaro, some animals thrive. I'm a Hooded Oriole, and I'm trying to find my friends who are hidden because of their natural camouflage.

Find a desert iguana, a roadrunner, a kit fox, a horned lizard, a kangaroo rat, a jackrabbit, a leopard lizard, and an elf owl. If you help me, I'll have it made in the (phew!) shade.

Illustrated by Marc Nadel

What's to Eat?

All sorts of carnivorous animals are hidden in this grid. Look across, backward, up, down, or diagonally as you search for each animal on the list. Once you've found them all, copy the leftover letters in order to discover what type of animal a carnivore is.

BADGER
BLACK BEAR
BOBCAT
CAT
COATI
COYOTE
DOG
ERMINE
FERRET
FISHER
GRAY FOX
GRIZZLY
LYNX
MARTIN
MINK
MOUNTAIN LION
OCELOT
OTTER
RACCOON
RED FOX
SEAL
TIMBER WOLF
WEASEL
WOLVERINE

X O F D E R E H S I F N
O W O L V E R I N E O I
F B M E N I M R E I T T
Y A L G R I Z Z L Y T R
A D I E E A T N R A E A
R G T T S O I A C S R M
G E A B L A C K B E A R
L R O E T C E O E A A K
Y T C N O G E W Y L R N
N O U O O T A C B O B I
X O N D T E R R E F T M
M F L O W R E B M I T E

A carnivore is a __________ ___________.

When I Grow Up

What will each of these animal babies be when it grows up?

1. fawn
2. calf
3. colt
4. cygnet
5. gosling
6. lamb
7. kid
8. tadpole
9. duckling
10. joey

Answers on page 138.

Meg's Magical Mystery Paint

Meg the Magician volunteered to paint the signs for the animal cages at the zoo. But she used her Magical Mystery Paint, and part of each word disappeared! See if you can figure out what the animal names are.

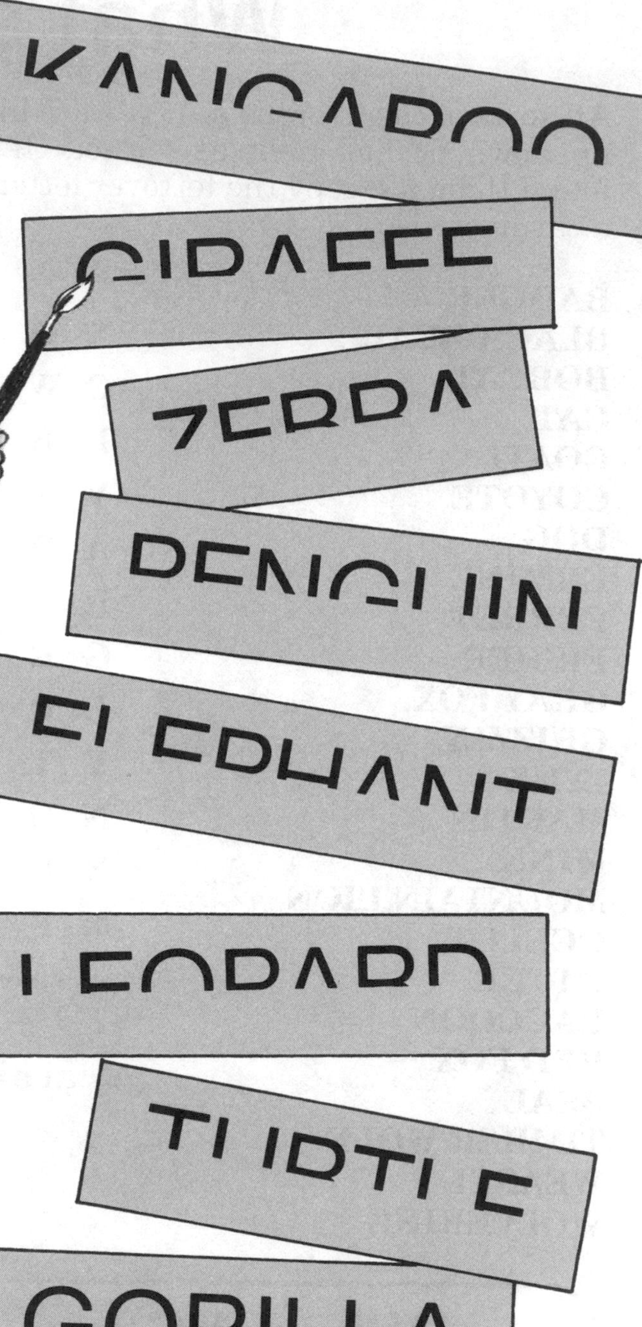

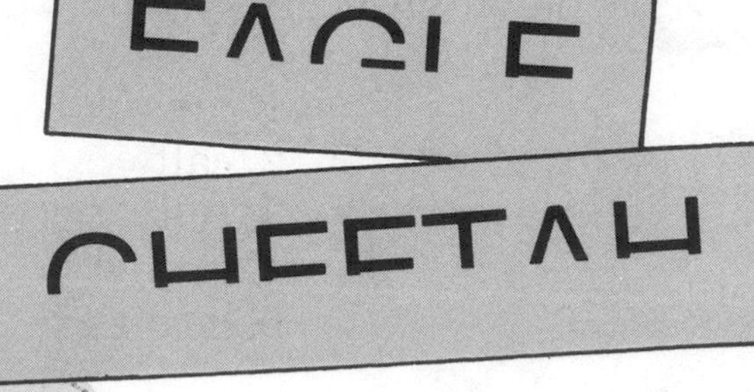

The answers appear on page 138.

Animal Cutouts

In the large picture below find the frog, turtle, giraffe, opossum, armadillo, panda, monkey, zebra, skunk, peacock, bat, porcupine, camel, alligator, penguin, hippopotamus, parrot, butterfly, seal, and the heads of a lion, a rhinoceros, a goat, and an elephant.

Illustrated by Melissa Crane

Sing a Little Tuna

Use the code key below to find out what song the cats on the fence are singing.

CODE KEY

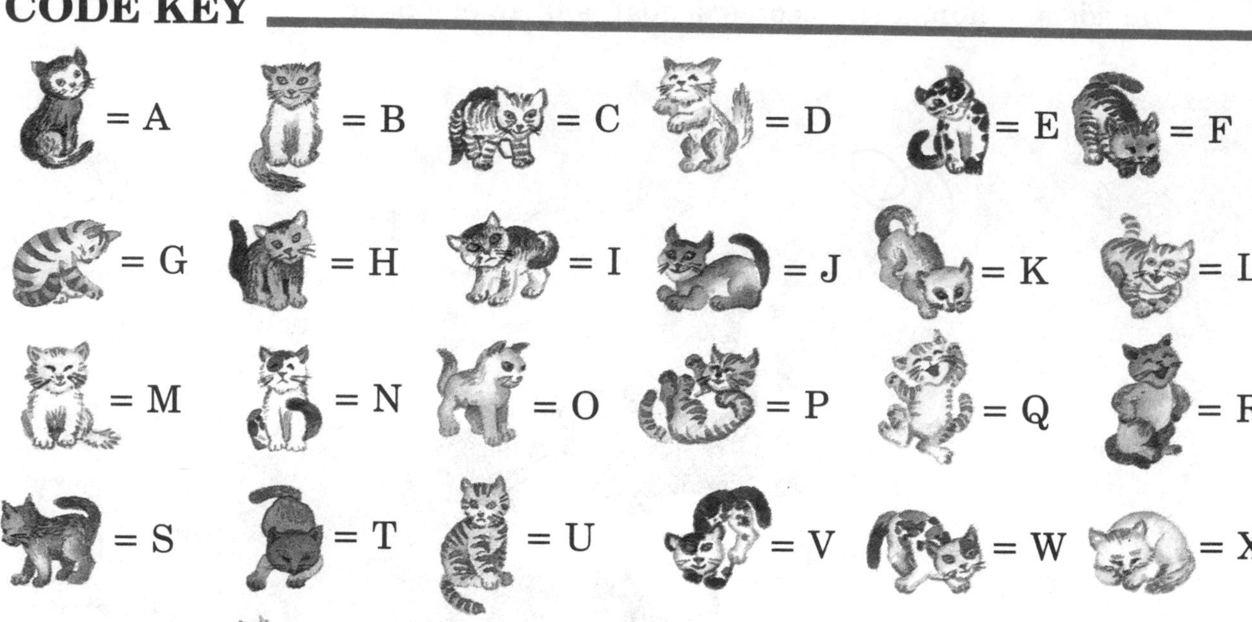

Wanna Bet?

If it takes 10 minutes to make one hard-boiled egg, how long does it take to make 10 hard-boiled eggs?

Hightail it to page 138 for the answers.

DOUBLED DRAGONS

Which two dragons match?

ANT ANTICS

A cherry dropped by Picnic Pete has fallen beneath the tall grasses. Can you help Andy Ant find it for his supper?

Answers on page 138.

Packing Up

Can you find at least twelve differences between these two pictures?

Late Again

Illustrated by Carlos Garzón

RIDDLE RHYMES

1. If you don't know this,
   You can tell me later.
   How can you tell when an elephant
   Is in the refrigerator?

2. What do you get,
   Now you tell me,
   When you cross an elephant
   With a bumblebee?

3. Why is it an elephant
   Never fails
   To put red polish
   On its nails?

4. I know you like to swim,
   Especially when it's hot.
   But how can you tell that elephants
   Like to swim a lot?

5. What do you get when you trip
   And make an elephant fall
   While taking a crate of oranges
   To the local shopping mall?

6. What time would it be
   If one or two
   Elephants got
   Into bed with you?

Answers on page 138.

Illustrated by Anthony Rao

Port of Call

Before coming to America, Christopher Columbus visited one of the islands below. Now these three explorers would like to recreate that event. Using the clues, can you help them figure out which island Columbus visited?

The island has a stream.

The island does not have a jungle.

There is more than one peak on this island, but none of them is a volcano.

Illustrated by Terry Rogers

Sail to page 138 for the answer.

Continental Drift

Can you find the name of a country hidden somewhere in each sentence below?

Example: **Fran ce**lebrated her eighth birthday last week.

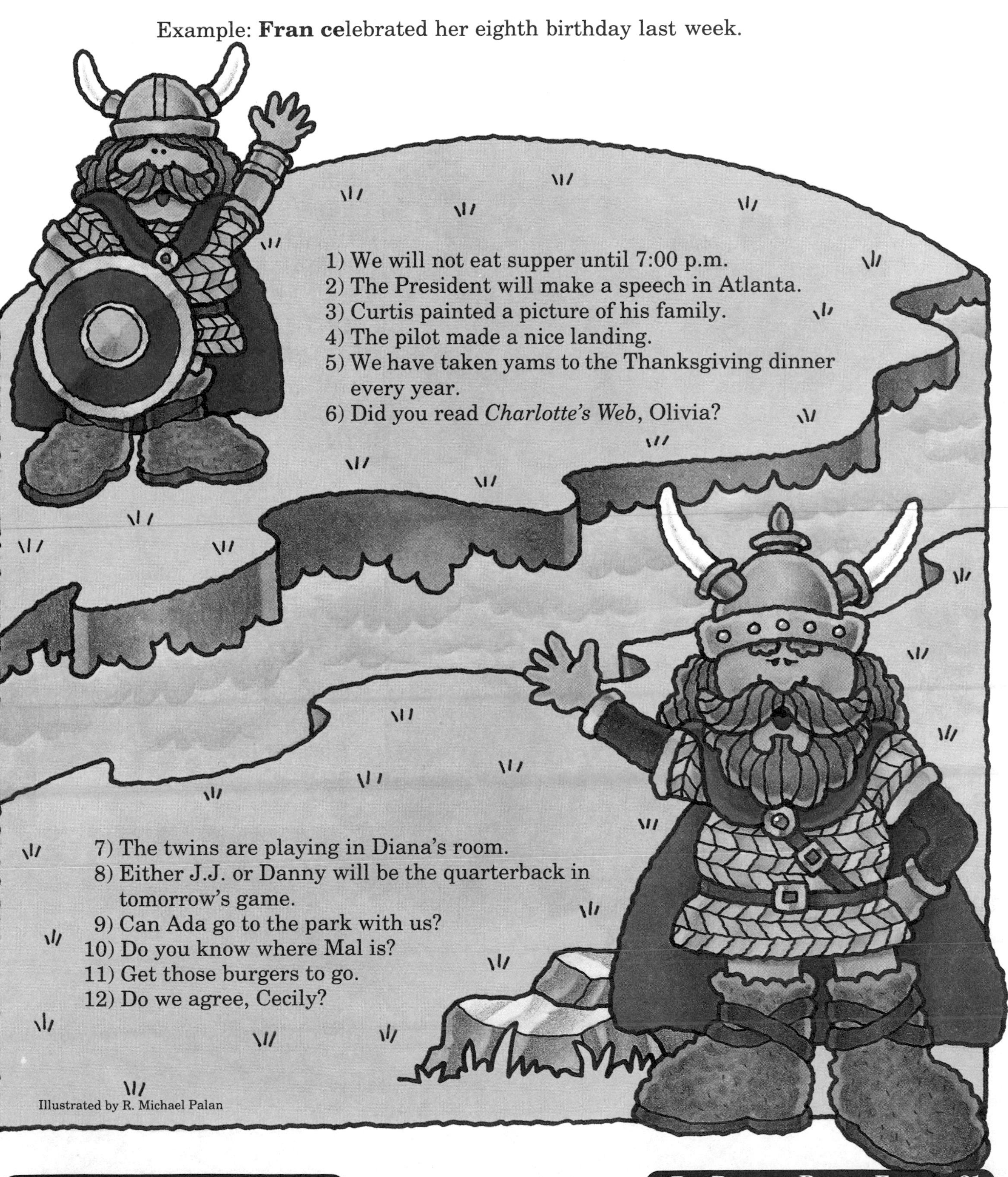

1) We will not eat supper until 7:00 p.m.
2) The President will make a speech in Atlanta.
3) Curtis painted a picture of his family.
4) The pilot made a nice landing.
5) We have taken yams to the Thanksgiving dinner every year.
6) Did you read *Charlotte's Web*, Olivia?
7) The twins are playing in Diana's room.
8) Either J.J. or Danny will be the quarterback in tomorrow's game.
9) Can Ada go to the park with us?
10) Do you know where Mal is?
11) Get those burgers to go.
12) Do we agree, Cecily?

Illustrated by R. Michael Palan

Travel to page 139 for the answers.

Mountain Match

Scale to new heights by matching each of these famous mountains to the country or state where it is located.

FUJI ____________
EVEREST ____________
RUSHMORE ____________
KILIMANJARO ____________
McKINLEY ____________
MONT BLANC ____________
MATTERHORN ____________
SHASTA ____________
PIKE'S PEAK ____________
ETNA ____________

Tanzania, Africa
France, Europe
California, North America
Italy, Europe
Nepal, Asia
Colorado, North America
South Dakota, North America
Japan, Asia
Alaska, North America
Switzerland, Europe

Answers on page 139.

Strings and Rings Magic

For this magic trick, you'll need a piece of string about two feet long, two bangle bracelets exactly alike, and a long-sleeve shirt or sweatshirt with a pocket in the front.

To prepare for the trick, wear the shirt and push the sleeves up so they are fairly bulky. Put one of the bracelets on and push it up your arm so it is hidden under the folds of your shirt sleeve.

To perform the trick, ask someone in the audience to tie one end of the string to your left wrist and the other end to your right wrist. Hold up the other bangle bracelet so the audience can see it, but don't let them see the one hidden in your sleeve.

Turn your back toward the audience or have an assistant hold a blanket up in front of you. Quickly hide the bracelet you showed the audience in your shirt pocket. Pull the bracelet from under your sleeve, down your arm, and onto the middle of the string.

Turn back to your audience or have your assistant whisk away the blanket. The audience will be amazed when they see that your wrists are still tied but the bracelet is hanging from the middle of the string.

Take your bow, clever magician!

Moving Mountains

Stare at the figure below. What do you see? Do you see dark mountains moving around? Or light triangles pointing down? Or maybe you see squares? Continue staring at the figure, and you may see moving, changing shapes and figures!

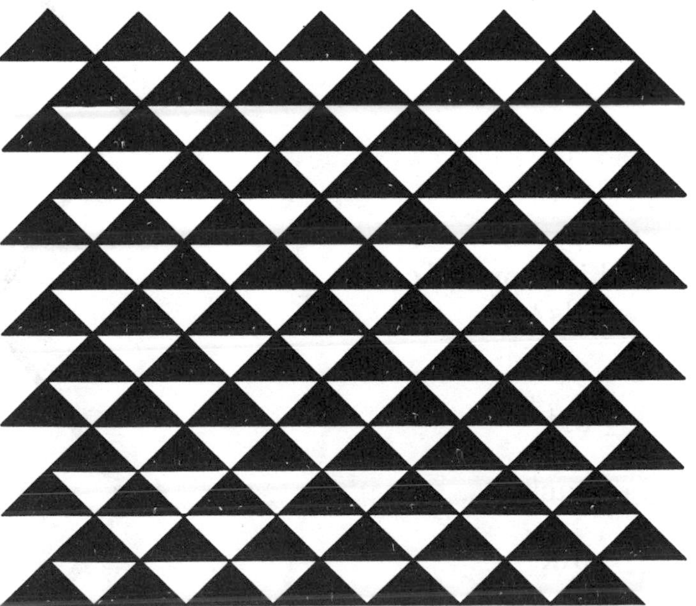

Square 'Em Up!

Cut a piece of paper into eight identical paper squares. Cut four of the squares in half diagonally so you have a total of eight triangles.

Put the four uncut squares and the eight triangles together in such a way that they form one big square.

Word Wise

1. One word in this sentence is spelled incorrectally. Which word is it?

2. How many months have 28 days in them?

3. Match each line with the word that describes it.

horizontal   vertical   diagonal   crooked   angled

4. What do H, I, and M have in common that they don't share with S, B, or O?

5. What do H, I, S, and O have in common that they don't share with M, A, or T?

6. What single letter can be placed in front of each word below to create six new words?

____ roof	____ art
____ roper	____ each
____ age	____ ink
____ rice	____ ear

Answers on page 139.

Magna-Search

Look carefully at the puzzle below. Every time you find the words *red, hose, nozzle, no, fire,* or *wrench,* color them in red. Many words will appear more than once. Can you help the firefighter find what he is looking for?

Illustrated by McKenzie Perrin

Answers on page 139.

MONEY MATTER$

Dotty and Rita went shopping at the Smart Money Market. After looking at the scene, can you answer the questions about their shopping?

1. If Rita bought a jump rope, a box of markers, and a soccer ball, what's the smallest single bill she could use to pay for them all?

2. Dotty likes coins because they remind her of metal dots. Before coming to the store, she counted up all her money. She has twenty-three pennies, eight nickels, six dimes, ten quarters, and four half dollars. If there is no tax, what one object does Dotty have exactly enough money to buy?

3. If the girls buy a pack of cards, two candy bars, and two quilt magazines, how much change will they get back from $10?

Tape Time

If I want to record all the songs below onto one tape, what's the shortest length tape I'll need: 45 minutes, 60 minutes, 75 minutes, or 90 minutes?

Side 1

Title	Artist	Length
Puzzle Bop	Big Jay's Orchestra	3:42
Peace in the World	Pam and the Wonder Wheel	4:16
Recycle Now	Wild Rose	2:52
Raleigh's Leg	Timmy Gee	7:30
We Are the Penguins	The Dancing Robs	5:21
Down on My Farm	Kay Brown	3:35
Theme from "Vanguard"	Christine and Jose	6:08

Side 2

Title	Artist	Length
Outer Space Race	Little Greg	4:29
Way Out Front	MGA	1:54
Do It Right	Korbs Hammer	6:33
Bus Stop Blues	Tray-Zee	5:55
Monkey Mask	Jan Can	3:12
Phantom	Avatar	6:47
Ice Cream Someday	Beth-Beth	4:08

Answers on page 139.

Clipped Coupons

Clara clipped some coupons for her shopping trip, but she accidentally cut off the names of the products. Match each product name with the coupon from which it was clipped.

1. Juicy Watermelon
2. All Right Orange Juice
3. Grade A Eggs
4. Bruno Brand Chickens
5. Barney's Bagels
6. MooCow Milk
7. Fresh Carrots

(A)
Locally Grown $.25/lb.
Vine-Ripened!

(B)
Fresh–from the Coop
to You! One Dozen
Free with Purchase of
$10.00 in Groceries

(C)
Farm Fresh
Buy a Carton, Get a
Carton FREE

(D)
Sold by the Dozen Only
Buy a Dozen, Get 1 Free
Fresh Today!
No Preservatives

(E)
5 lb./$1.00
Reg. $25/lb
Locally Grown

(F)
Buy it by the Gallon or the
Half-Gallon
Fresh-Squeezed Today!
No Pulp!

(G)
Roasters De-Boned
Buy Now and Get a FREE
Recipe Booklet:
"100 Possibilities with
Poultry"

Wrong Ring-Up

Which cash register isn't totaling properly?

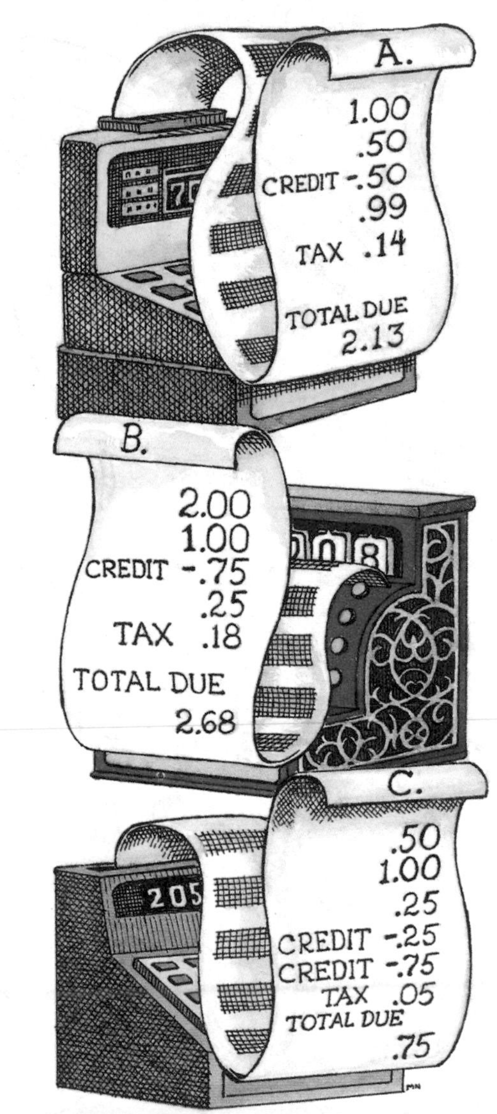

A.
1.00
.50
CREDIT -.50
.99
TAX .14
TOTAL DUE
2.13
B.
2.00
1.00
CREDIT -.75
.25
TAX .18
TOTAL DUE
2.68
C.
.50
1.00
.25
CREDIT -.25
CREDIT -.75
TAX .05
TOTAL DUE
.75

Side Stack

Which is the correct side view of the disks stacked here?

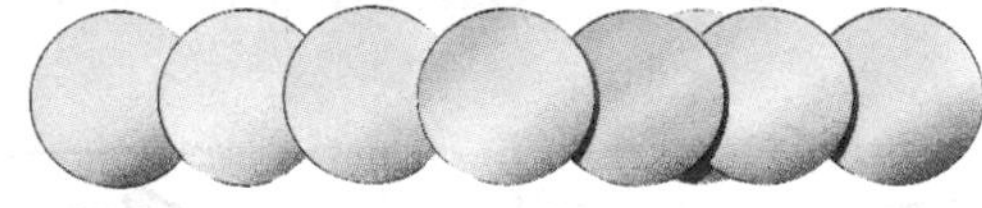

A. 

B. 

C. 

D. 

E. 

F. 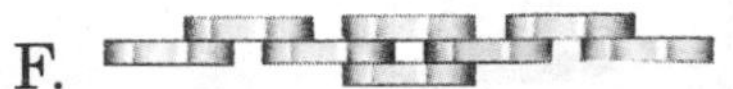

Answers on page 139.

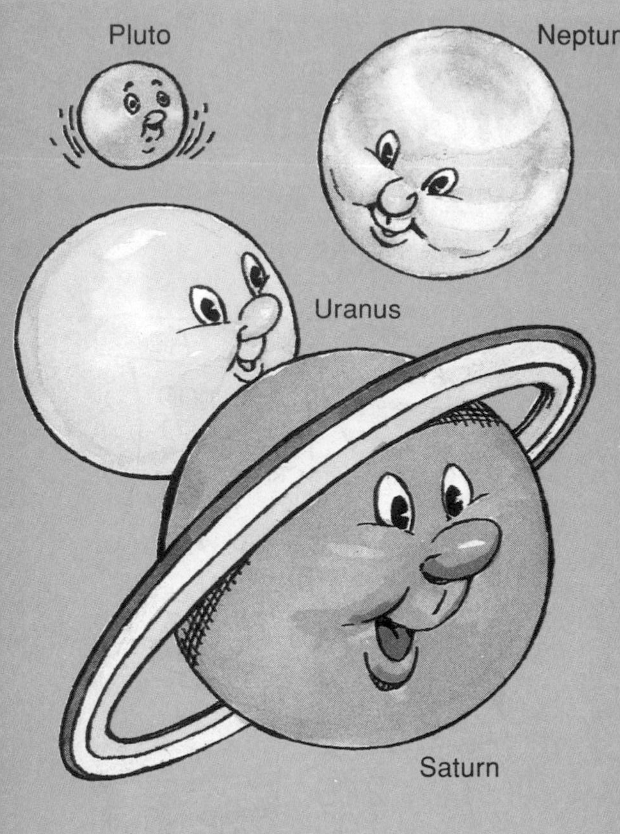

You're Invited

Match each invitation to a planet.

1. I may be small, but I'm farthest from you,
   So come visit me for a great galactic view.
2. I'm next to the sun, and you'd like a lot
   To visit me if you want to be HOT.
3. Don't mind that I'm named for the god of war.
   Come visit me. I'm just out your back door.
4. Come visit me, for days short and sweet.
   More than that, I'm the biggest you'll meet.
5. We all have our charms with our colors and things,
   But nobody else has my wonderful rings.
6. I'm nearest to you, so my claims come above
   All the others. Besides, I'm the goddess of love.
7. I'm named for the god who ruled the sea.
   So sail your ship through space to me.
8. Not too near, too far, too big, or too small,
   And there's "us" in me, so come one and all.
9. If it should be that you choose not to roam,
   Take care of me, please, your beautiful home.

Illustrated by Marc Nadel

Unearthly Hares

What words do each of these pictures represent?

1.
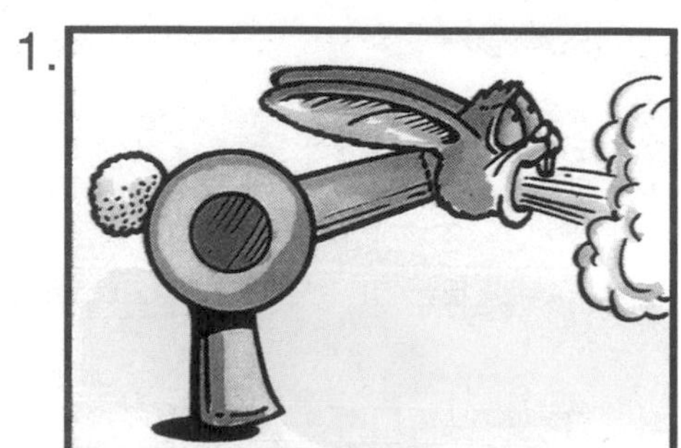

2.

3.

Illustrated by Joe Seidita

Answers on page 139.

PLANET PALS

These are just some of the creatures the Pals met while traveling through space. Can you match each alien with its proper planet?

A

F

1

2

3

E

4

Jeff

B

6

5

D

C

Illustrated by Leslie Harris

The planets are paired on page 139.

AT FRIDAY'S FOOTWEAR

WE HAVE ONE SIMPLE MOTTO THAT STANDS BEHIND EVERY SHOE WE SELL

T.G.I.F.

TOES GO IN FIRST

1/2 OFF

MAPIMAJULASN

SUNDAY	MONDAY	TUESDAY	WEDNESDAY	THURSDAY	FRIDAY	SATURDAY
Each date on this calendar is correctly labeled with a holiday. Unfortunately, no one is sure in what month each holiday belongs. See if you can write the correct month in the date given for each holiday.				1 NEW YEAR'S DAY	2 GROUNDHOG DAY	3
4 INDEPENDENCE DAY	5 LABOR DAY	6 ELECTION DAY	7 HANUKKAH	8 ROSH HASHANAH	9 GOOD FRIDAY	10
11 MOTHER'S DAY	12 COLUMBUS DAY	13	14 VALENTINE'S DAY	15 MARTIN LUTHER KING'S BIRTHDAY	16	17 ST. PATRICK'S DAY
18 FATHER'S DAY	19 PRESIDENTS' DAY	20 FIRST DAY OF SPRING	21 ASH WEDNESDAY	22 THANKSGIVING	23	24
25 CHRISTMAS	26 MEMORIAL DAY	37	28	29 PASSOVER	30	31 HALLOWEEN

Answers on page 139.

Fun Days

Terry was trying to arrange her calendar for a month of fun when she realized that a month's worth of words could be made from the letters in CALENDAR. Using these letters, can you fill in the word described on each day of this calendar? The first one has been done for you.

CALENDAR

Sunday	Monday	Tuesday	Wednesday	Thursday	Friday	Saturday
		1 genuine *real*	2 a walking stick	3 to mend a hole	4 ground	5 not dirty
6 run swiftly	7 a rocking baby's bed	8 not far away	9 to guide	10 a narrow roadway	11 a playing card with only one symbol	12 to challenge
13 a young boy	14 bargain or agreement	15 a deck of ______ s	16 an arched gallery of shops	17 not cloudy	18 rhythmic movements	19 to gain knowledge
20 beloved or precious	21 a lion's lair	22 wax mold with a wick	23 ______ a book	24 a tall wading bird	25 to offer and give temporarily	26 concern
27 the fat of a pig	28 a design made to be transferred	29 a long, sharp knight's weapon	30 to finish	31 watery passageway in Panama		

Make a date to check the answers on page 139.

Spring Things

All the words below are about spring. Use the size of each word as a clue to fit it into the right spaces on the grid. Some words may go together in different ways, but all the words will fit in only one unique design.

7 Letters

Rainbow

8 Letters

Passover

Sunshine

4 Letters

Eggs

Leaf

Nest

Play

Rain

Thaw

Trip

Warm

5 Letters

Grass

Green

Worms

3 Letters

Ice

Mud

Toy

6 Letters

Easter

Flower

Insect

Puddle

Spring

Answers on page 139.

A Topsy-Turvy Train Ride
How many unusual things can you find in this picture?
TICKETS
TISSUE
M. Nadel

Colorful Names

Can you match each name to the color it represents?

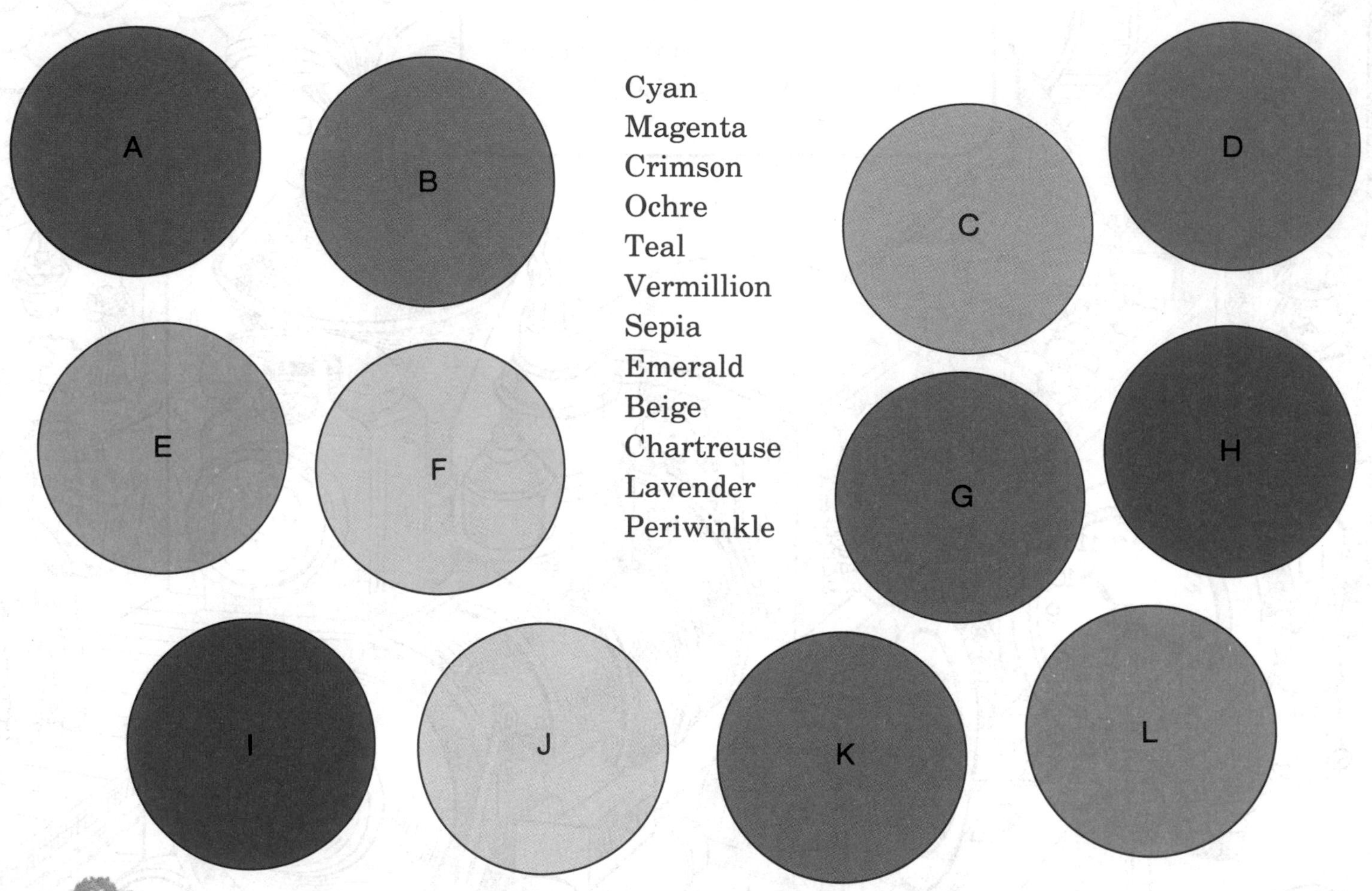

Cyan
Magenta
Crimson
Ochre
Teal
Vermillion
Sepia
Emerald
Beige
Chartreuse
Lavender
Periwinkle

Whose Flower Is That?

Scientists who study plants sometimes name new ones to honor special people. Guess which flowering plant was named for each of these people.

gardenia	1. Pierre Magnol, French botanist
magnolia	2. Joel Robert Poinsett, U.S. minister to Mexico
forsythia	3. Johann Gottfried Zinn, German botanist
poinsettia	4. Georg Josef Camel, missionary to the Philippines
zinnia	5. Michel Begon, French government official
dahlia	6. William Forsythe, English botanist
begonia	7. Anders Dahl, Swedish botanist
camellia	8. Alexander Garden, Scottish physician and naturalist

Answers on page 139.

Rhyme Time

Fill in the blanks with words you can make from letters in the word ELEPHANT. If you fill in the right words, each two-sentence verse will rhyme. The first one is done for you.

1. Another word for jump is LEAP.
Another word for pile is HEAP.

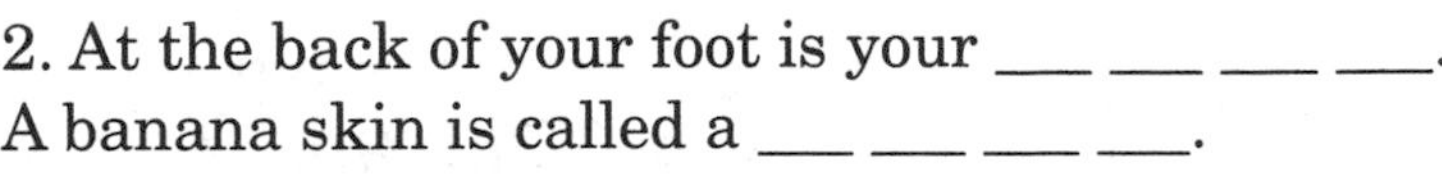

2. At the back of your foot is your ___ ___ ___ ___.
A banana skin is called a ___ ___ ___ ___.

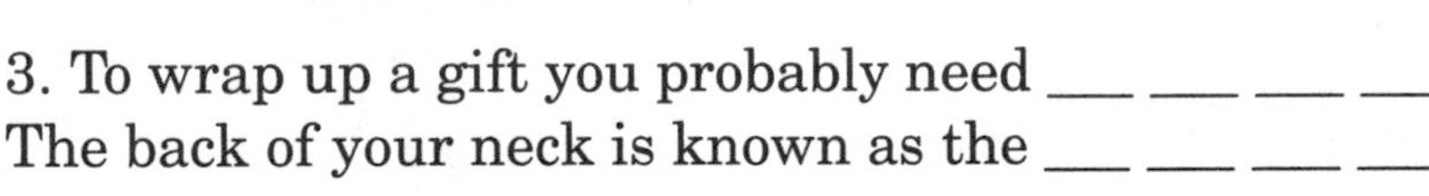

3. To wrap up a gift you probably need ___ ___ ___ ___.
The back of your neck is known as the ___ ___ ___ ___.

4. Your parents like you to keep your room ___ ___ ___ ___.
When winter comes, most houses need ___ ___ ___ ___.

5. What two-letter combination can you use to fill in the blanks below so that the rhyme is complete? (Hint: The same combination is used every time.)

When my ___ ___eepdog ___ ___ook after his swampy swim,
I _ _ould have kept away from him.
My ___ ___irt and ___ ___orts and ___ ___oes got wet.
Go___ ___, will Mother be upset!
___ ___e'll sniff at me and hold her nose,
Then make me wa___ ___ and change my clothes.

How many rhyming words can you make by dropping the first letter of each word below and replacing it with a new one? We've started the first one for you.

mill	book	sink	mad	bake
bill				
hill				
pill				
fill				
will				
dill				
gill				
till				
sill				

Answers on page 139.

Fortune Hunting

It's time for dessert. But you can't eat these fortune cookies until you can match the two cookies that make a complete fortune. For example, if the first half of a fortune reads "A stitch in time...," the matching half will say "saves nine."

...ALWAYS GOES BAREFOOT
A MONEYLESS MAN...
A GOLDEN KEY...
THE SHOEMAKER'S SON...
...BEGINS WITH JUST A SINGLE STEP
YOU CANNOT PUT AN OLD HEAD...
...CAN OPEN ANY DOOR.
...GOES FAST THROUGH THE MARKET
...CATCHES NO MICE
IF YOU CAN'T RIDE TWO HORSES...
YOU STAY WITH THE GIRL...
...DOES NOT CHANGE HIS SPOTS
...YOU SHOULDN'T BE IN THE CIRCUS
THE LEOPARD...
A CAT WHO WEARS GLOVES...
...ON YOUNG SHOULDERS
...YOU BROUGHT TO THE DANCE
A JOURNEY OF 1,000 MILES...

Match your fortunes on page 140.

Cog Clog

Rambyte, the Puzzle Pal's compact computer, slipped some springs and popped some cogs. Now Holly and Molly are looking through the spare parts to find a matching set of springs and a matching pair of cogs so they can fix Rambyte. Can you help locate each pair of matching parts?

Answers on page 140.

Riddle Me These

Figure out the punch lines of these riddles in order to fill in the squares of this "cross-mirth" puzzle. Don't be April Fooled and you'll have some great jokes to tell your friends.

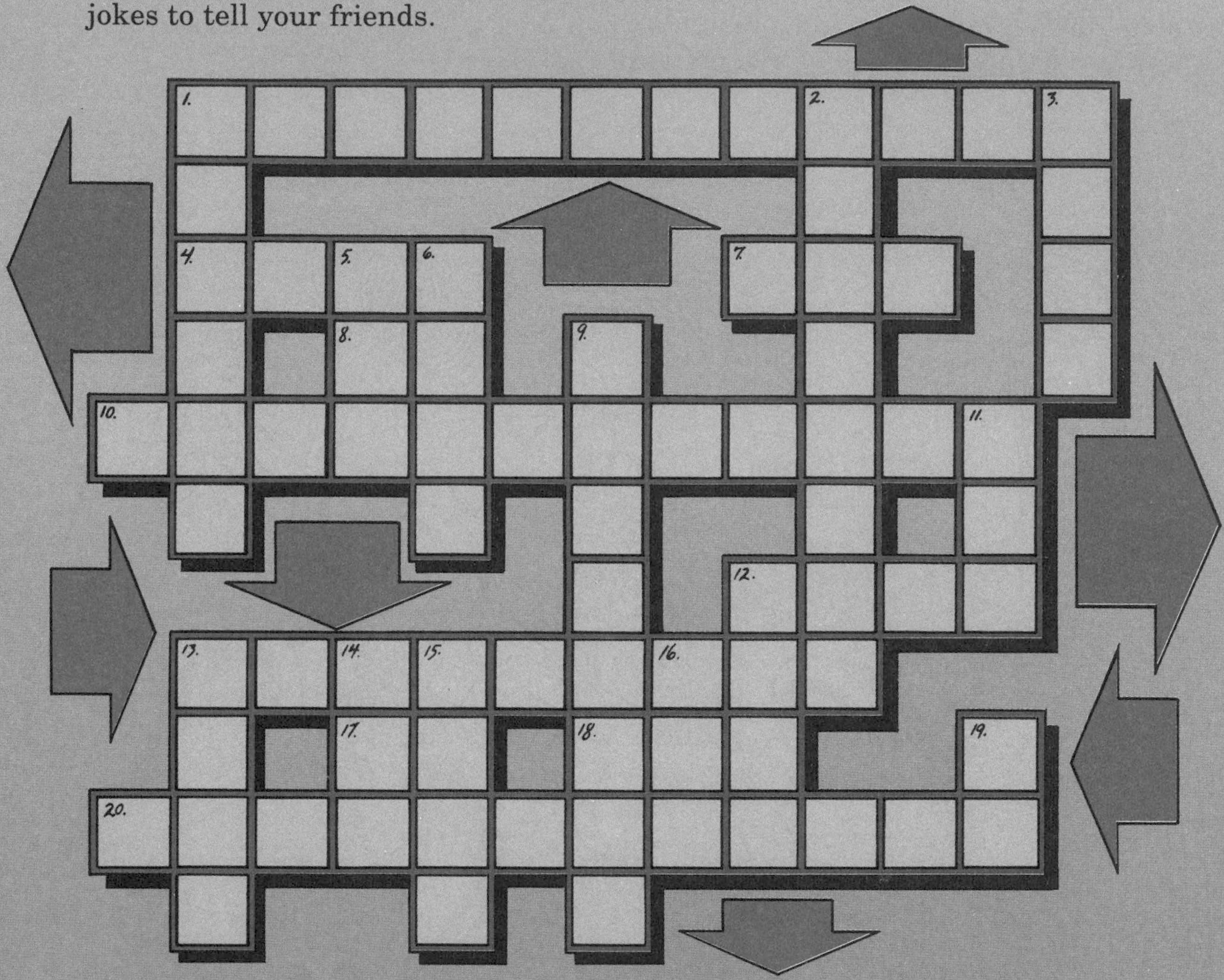

1. 2. 3. 4. 5. 6. 7. 8. 9. 10. 11. 12. 13. 14. 15. 16. 17. 18. 19. 20.

DOWN

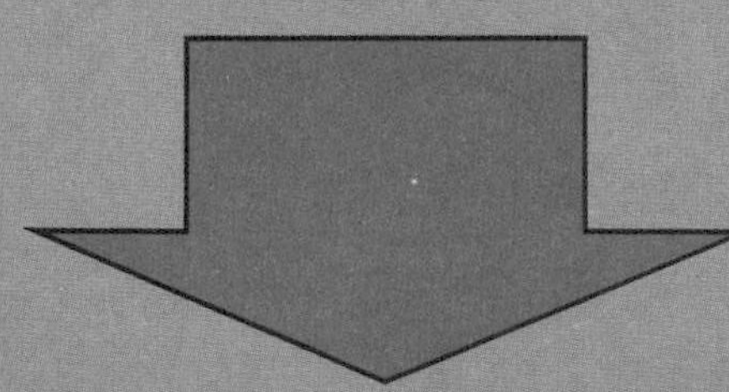

1. Which country reminds you of Thanksgiving?

2. What kind of ear does a train have? (ans.) An ____________.

3. What does a better job when it sleeps? (ans.) A __________.

5. Where might people stay when they go "out"? (ans.) An _________.

6. What should you always stop if it's running? (ans.) Your __________.

9. What's the best material for kites?

11. What animal would be likely to eat a relative? (ans.) An _______ eater.

12. What fruit sounds like two but is really just one? (ans.) A __________.

13. What name is always mentioned in church?

14. What catches flies better than Daryl Strawberry? (ans.) A __________.

15. Why is the sun brighter in Hollywood? (ans.) Because it's a _________.

16. When is a dog not a dog? (ans.) When it's a ____________.

19. What two letters always turn out good?

Get in on the laughs on page 140.

Buying A Bonnet

Sally needs to buy a new bonnet for Easter. Use the clues to decide which hat she will buy.

Sally likes ribbons, but not dots.

Her favorite color is yellow, but she'll never wear blue or red.

Illustrated by Paul Richer

ACROSS

1. Why did the man throw the clock out the window?

4. What kind of bow cannot be tied? (ans.) A ________ bow.

7. What goes up and never comes down?

8. What are the least obliging two letters in the alphabet?

10. What's the biggest pencil in the world?

12. What did Mrs. Moss name her only son?

13. What's black and white and read all over? (ans.) A ________.

17. Who has the biggest phone bill in the galaxy?

18. What's the only letter you can eat?

20. What has four wheels and flies? (ans.) A ________ ________.

"Open it wider. . . wider. . . still wider."

Head to page 140 for the answer.

Brain Teasers

1. What is the plural of sheep?
2. Which is correct: 8+7 is 14 or 8+7 are 14?
3. What letter comes next in the sequence: T W T F ___ ?
4. Which of these six words are verbs (actions words)? Which are nouns?
   CAT RUN BUILD MAN THINK FROG

What is the incorrect detail in each story below?

5. "Tomorrow is the day of the annual toboggan races," Jeff told Matthew. "I'm going to watch the races with my dad."

   "I can't go this year," Matthew said, "but I'm going to watch them on TV tonight."

6. "Grandma," Eddie cried. "I lost my mitten."
   "Let's look for it," Grandma told him.
   They looked everywhere--in closets, on all the shelves, even in the shoe box. Then Eddie checked the "lost-and-found" box at school.
   "It's not there either," he said when he came home from school.
   "Don't worry," Grandma smiled. "Look. I already started knitting you a new hat."

7. Don the Detective followed the suspect's brown car as it slowed down and stopped at the green light. He saw the missing poodle jump and lick the back window right before the light turned red and the car sped off.

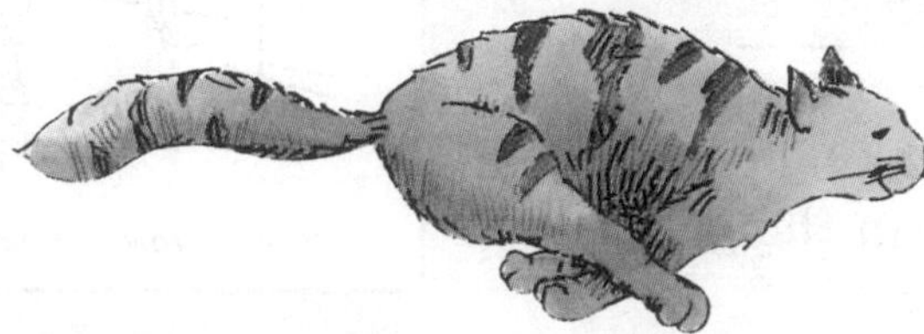

Answers on page 140.

Mum's the Word

"April showers bring May flowers" is a famous quote. To learn which flowers April brought, put together the sounds of Rebus Rita's pictures.

1 + __________

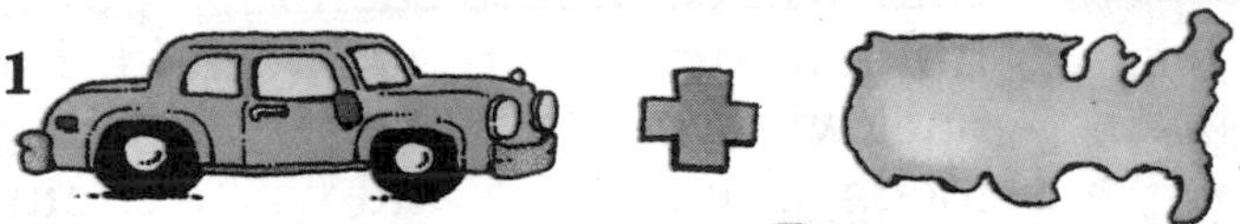

2 __________

3 + __________

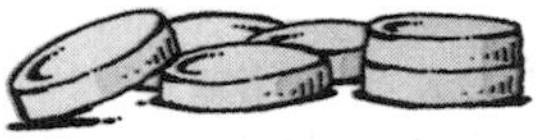

4 + + OLAS __________

5 V + + O + __________

6 + __________

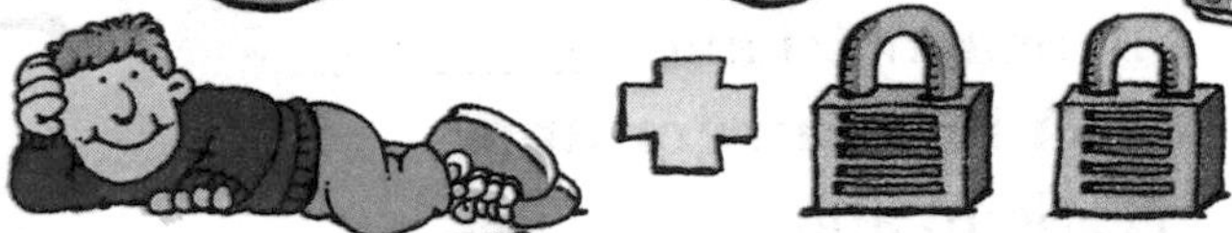

7 + + + __________

Illustated by Mike Dammer

Setting Up Camp

These scenes are all mixed up. Can you put them in order from what happened first to what happened last?

A

B

C

D

E

F

Answers on page 140.

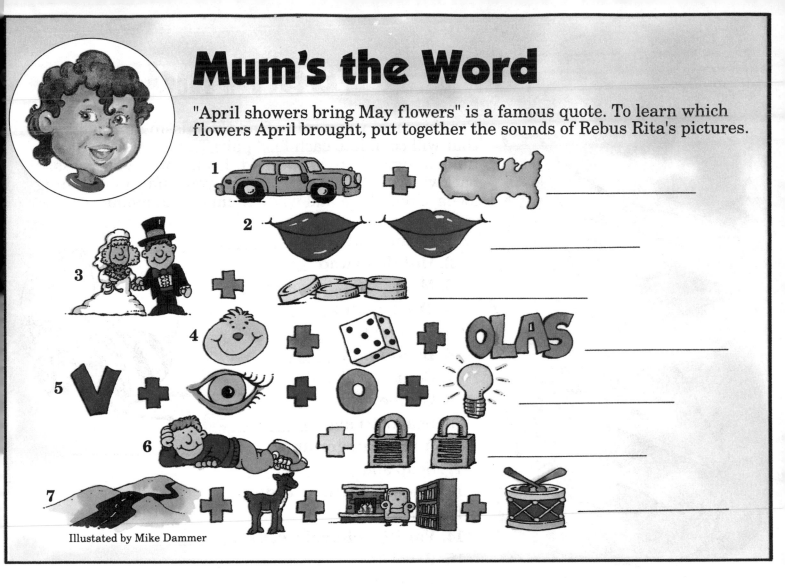

Food Find

For this meal you need to find the missing ingredients that will complete each food pair. The missing items are hidden somewhere in the grid. Look up, down, across, backward, and diagonally. When you find the matching foods, circle them and write them on the menu.

1. Peanut butter and ________
2. **Hot dogs and ________**
3. Mashed potatoes and ________
4. **Turkey and ________**
5. Milk and ________
6. **Bacon and ________**
7. Corned beef and ________
8. **Coffee and ________**
9. Spaghetti and ________
10. **A hamburger and ________ ________**
11. Soup and ________
12. **Bacon, lettuce, and ________**
13. Roll and ________
14. **Vanilla, chocolate, and ________**
15. Bagel and ________ ________
16. **Ham and ________**
17. Ice cream and ________
18. **Pancakes and ________**

C R E A M C H E E S E
S E I R F H C N E R F
L C T O T A M O T J Z
L R H E G A B B A C G
A A S C O O K I E S N
B C I A E G M F G O I
T K N K S J R T G I F
A E A E E B E A S T F
E R D L E S T L V O U
M S L A H W T U L Y T
V Y N Z C P U R Y S S
K S T R A W B E R R Y

Answers on page 140.

Vital Vittles

Some of the things we need for our lunch might be found among these groceries. Besides an egg and a bagel, find the book, snake, airplane, pig, house, number seven, baby bottle, canoe, elephant, fox's face, baby shoe, bowling ball, and train engine.

Breakfast Baffler

Mr. Toad can't figure out what to order. You can help him by placing each choice in the right spaces on his menu. Use the size of each word as a clue to see where it will fit.

3 Letters
EGG
HAM
JAM
TEA

4 Letters
BRAN
MILK
TART

5 Letters
BAGEL
BREAD
CREPE
FRUIT
HONEY
JELLY
JUICE
STEAK
SUGAR
TOAST

6 Letters
CEREAL
COFFEE
OMELET
PASTRY
WAFFLE
YOGURT

7 Letters
BISCUIT
~~MUFFINS~~
PANCAKE
SAUSAGE

MUFFINS

Fun Puns

What common word or phrase does each picture represent?

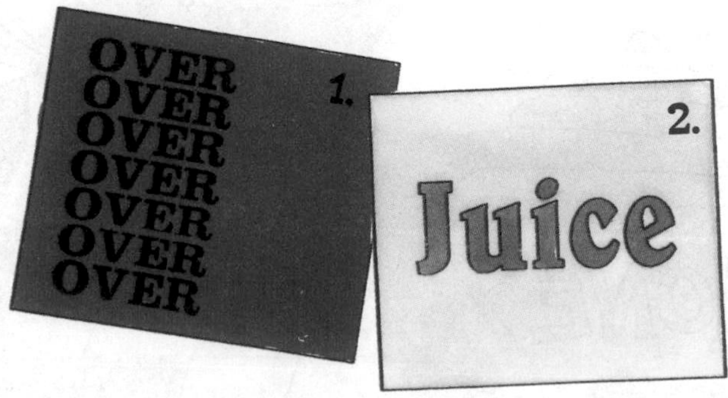

Answers on page 140.

Don't Be Negative

A.  B.  C. 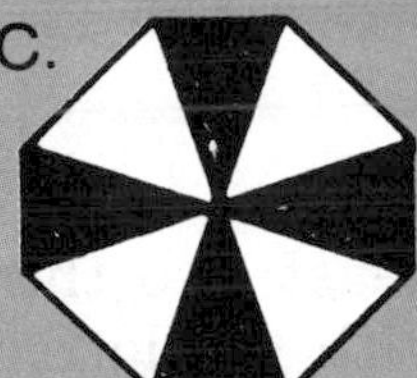 D. 

Four of these objects have the same design as four other objects. Only the colors have been reversed to show a negative image. Match up all four pairs.

E. 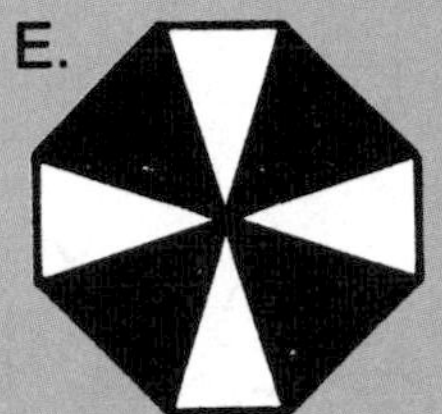 F. 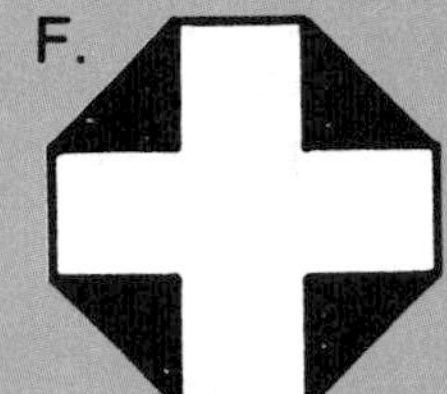 G.  H. 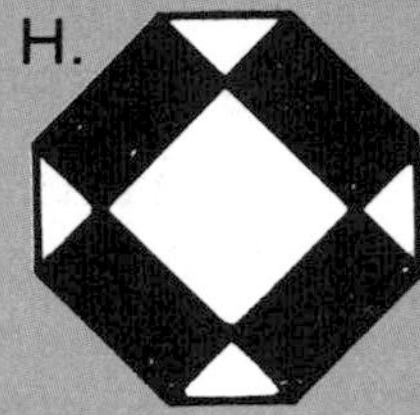

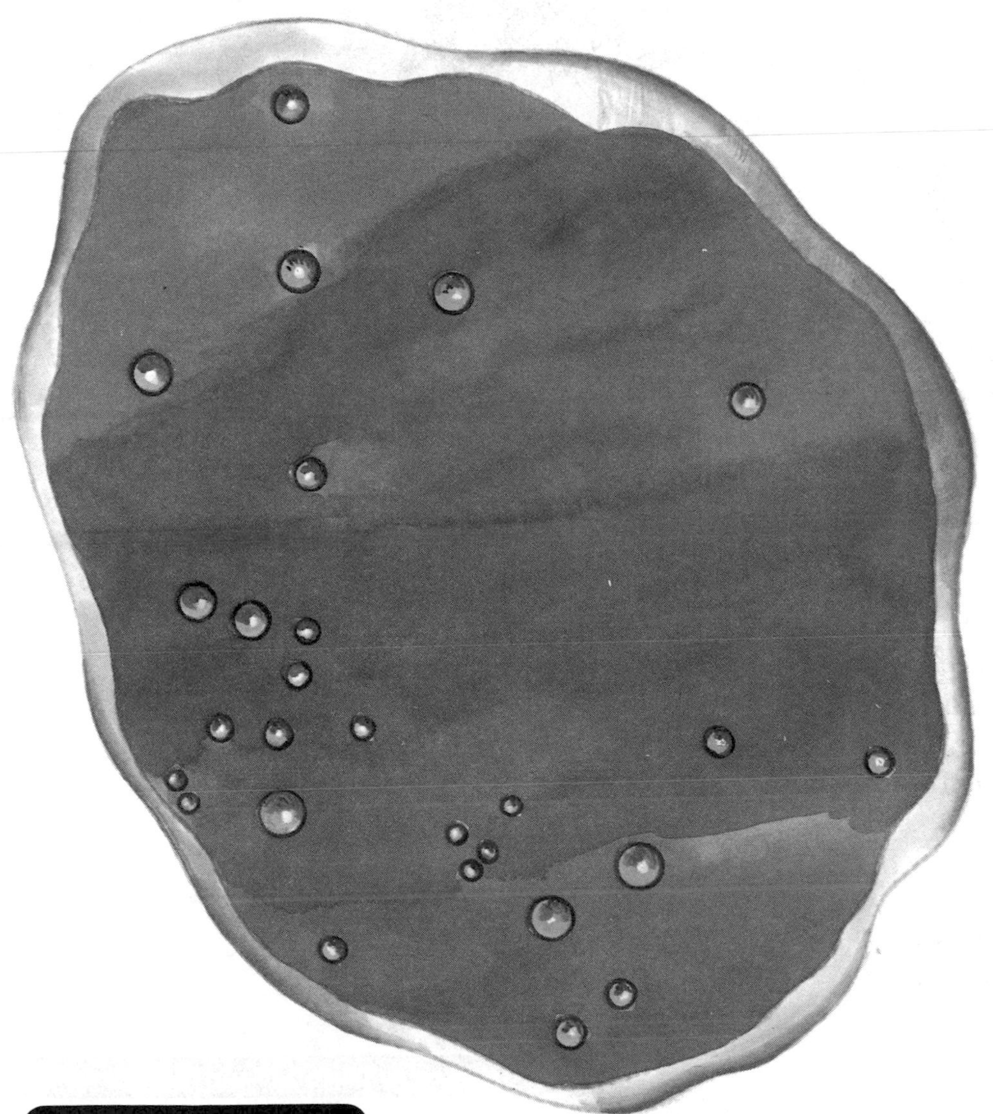

Pancake Puzzle

Miss Julie made a big mistake at breakfast today. Instead of making ten small pancakes, she made one giant one. Now she has to divide it into ten pieces with three blueberries on each piece. Her problem is that she's only allowed to use four straight lines to cut it. Can you solve her tasty problem?

Answers on page 140.

Perplexing Puzzles

Name at least two things that begin with the letter *P* for each category listed below. You will find some clues in the large picture at the right.

1. fruits
2. animals
3. flowers
4. vegetables
5. occupations
6. toys
7. clothing
8. school supplies

Put the correct vowels into the blanks of this familiar tongue twister. See how quickly you can say it three times.

P__t__r P__p__r p__ck__d a p__ck of p__ckl__d p__pp__rs.
A p__ck of p__ckl__d p__pp__rs P__t__r P__p__r p__cked.

Illustrated by Sue Parnell

Use the clues below to help you fill in the blanks of these double-p words.

1. you might polish this fruit — _ PP _ _
2. some pizzas have slices of this meat — _ _ PP _ _ _ _ _ _
3. the "legs" of a seal are called its — _ _ _ PP _ _ _
4. messy — _ _ _ PP _
5. a cat is to a kitten what a dog is to a — _ _ PP _
6. Tom Sawyer's river — _ _ _ _ _ _ _ _ _ _ PP _
7. hot and cold are; white and black are, too — _ PP _ _ _ _ _ _ _
8. he's not sad, he's — _ _ PP _
9. a word that means to clap your hands — _ PP _ _ _ _
10. an African animal often called a "river horse" — _ _ PP _ _ _ _ _ _ _ _ _

Pop over to page 140 for the answers.

Pass The P's, Please

How many things that begin with the letter *P* can you find in this picture?

Illustrated by Charles Jordan

Write the Headline

Read each sentence. If it is true, circle the blue letter under the letter ***T***. If it is false, circle the red letter under the letter ***F***.

Next, write the circled letters in order in the first twelve boxes. Then write the uncircled letters in order in the next twelve boxes. You will have a newspaper headline about Amelia Earhart.

		T	**F**
1.	New York City is by the ocean.	F	R
2.	A hot desert covers Maine.	O	I
3.	The Mississippi River flows into the Atlantic Ocean.	S	R
4.	The St. Lawrence River flows into the Atlantic.	S	S
5.	Puerto Rico is an island.	T	A
6.	Florida is always covered with snow.	T	W
7.	Washington, D.C. is east of Boston.	L	O
8.	Columbus sailed across the Atlantic Ocean.	M	A
9.	Paris is the capital of England.	N	A
10.	The Eiffel Tower is in London.	T	N
11.	Ireland has many lakes and mountains.	A	I
12.	Spain is further south than France.	C	C

Illustrated by Ron LeHew

1	2	3	4	5

6	7	8	9	10

11	12	1	2	3	4

5	6	7	8	9	10	11	12

Coin Exchange

Juan, Lelani, and Travis are on their way to Francie's Fresh Fruit stand. They've just emptied their piggy banks and found the coins shown at the right. They want to trade coins until all three of them have exactly the same amount of money. Can you show them how to do this by moving only two coins?

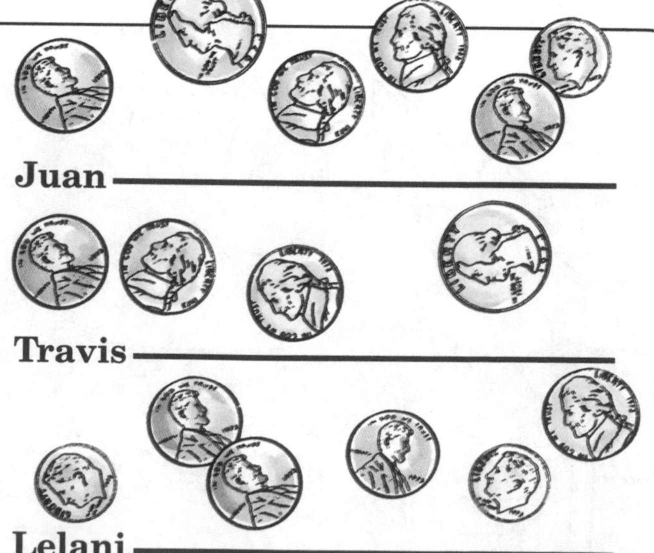

Answers on page 141.

Weather Words

1. Something about this old rhyme doesn't make sense. Can you figure out what it is ?

   March winds and April flowers
   Bring forth May showers.

2. All of the words below are different forms of some secret word that is hidden among them. Can you find it?

   d e w d r o p
   h a i l
   s t e a m
   i c e b e r g
   r a i n

3. This weatherman is having a problem figuring out his forecast. Change the first letter of each word and turn it into a weather term he can use for his forecast:

   funny
   pair
   fleet
   hold
   pain
   sail
   farm
   know

4. Find some weather words by answering each clue and then saying each set of three words together.

   A. One penny equals a ___ ___ ___ ___.
   A clock goes tock and ___ ___ ___ ___.
   The mark you get in school is your ___ ___ ___ ___ ___.

   B. To ride on a bus you must pay a ___ ___ ___ ___.
   If you're not out, you're ___ ___.
   How tall you are is called your ___ ___ ___ ___ ___ ___.

Answers on page 141.

Gone to the Dogs

The world-famous Iditarod dogsled race is about to begin. But Linc is missing again. He flew two thousand miles to see this event, and he'd hate to miss it. Can you find Linc before he gets lost?
Can you also find a penguin, a starfish, and a flower?

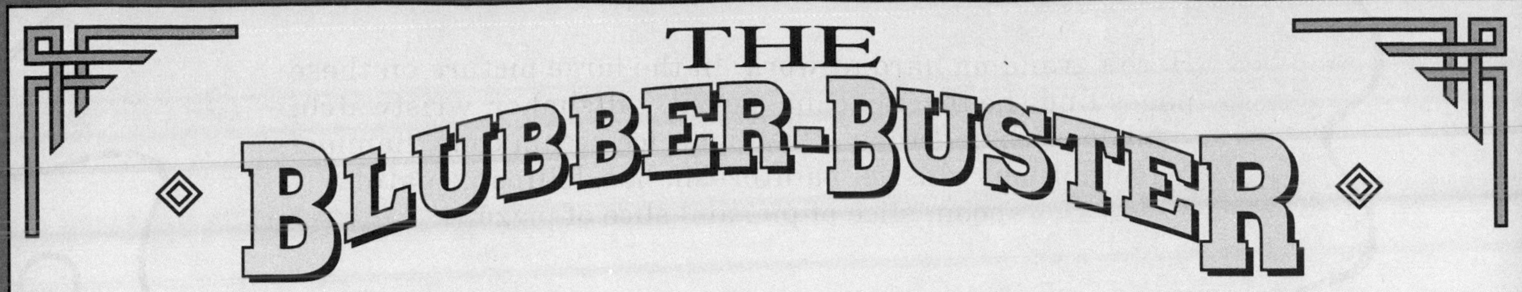

THE BLUBBER-BUSTER

You'll need to trim the blubber from these Alaskan animals to find their true names. The letters in the word BLUBBER have been mixed in with the name of each animal. Cross out the letters on each line as shown in the first example, then write the remaining letters in the spaces.

If you list each animal correctly, the boxed letters will give you the answer to the riddle below.

B̸L̸MU̸OB̸B̸OE̸SER̸ ☐ _ _ _ _

BLWUABLBREUSR _ ☐ _ _ _ _ _

PBLUYBGBMEYOWRL _ _ _ _ _ ☐ _ _ _ _

BCLAUBRIBBOEUR _ _ _ _ _ ☐ _ _

POBLURBCBUPEIRNE _ _ _ _ _ _ _ _ ☐

BLHUORBNEDBPEUFFIN _ _ _ _ _ ☐ _ _ _ _ _ _

MBLUOUBNBTAEINGORAT _ _ _ _ _ _ _ ☐ _ _ _ _ _

BLUCOBYBEORTE ☐ _ _ _ _ _

MBULUSBBKOEXR _ _ _ ☐ _ _

Who's the most indecisive whale in the world?

_ _ _ _ _ _ _ _ _ _ _ _

Answers on page 141.

Here's grandma hard at work. In the large picture on these pages find the teacup, cane, pencil, saltshaker, wristwatch, wishbone, whale, crown, flashlight, ice-cream cone, hammer, toothbrush, whistle, paintbrush, hat, lollipop, spatula, spoon, slice of pie, and slice of pizza.

HUGALICEOS

The title of this puzzle is a code word for "MOTHER'S DAY." Below are some famous moms, along with words about mothers that use the same code. Use the code to get as many letters as you can. Then try to fill in the remaining letters until you can complete this mom-umental list.

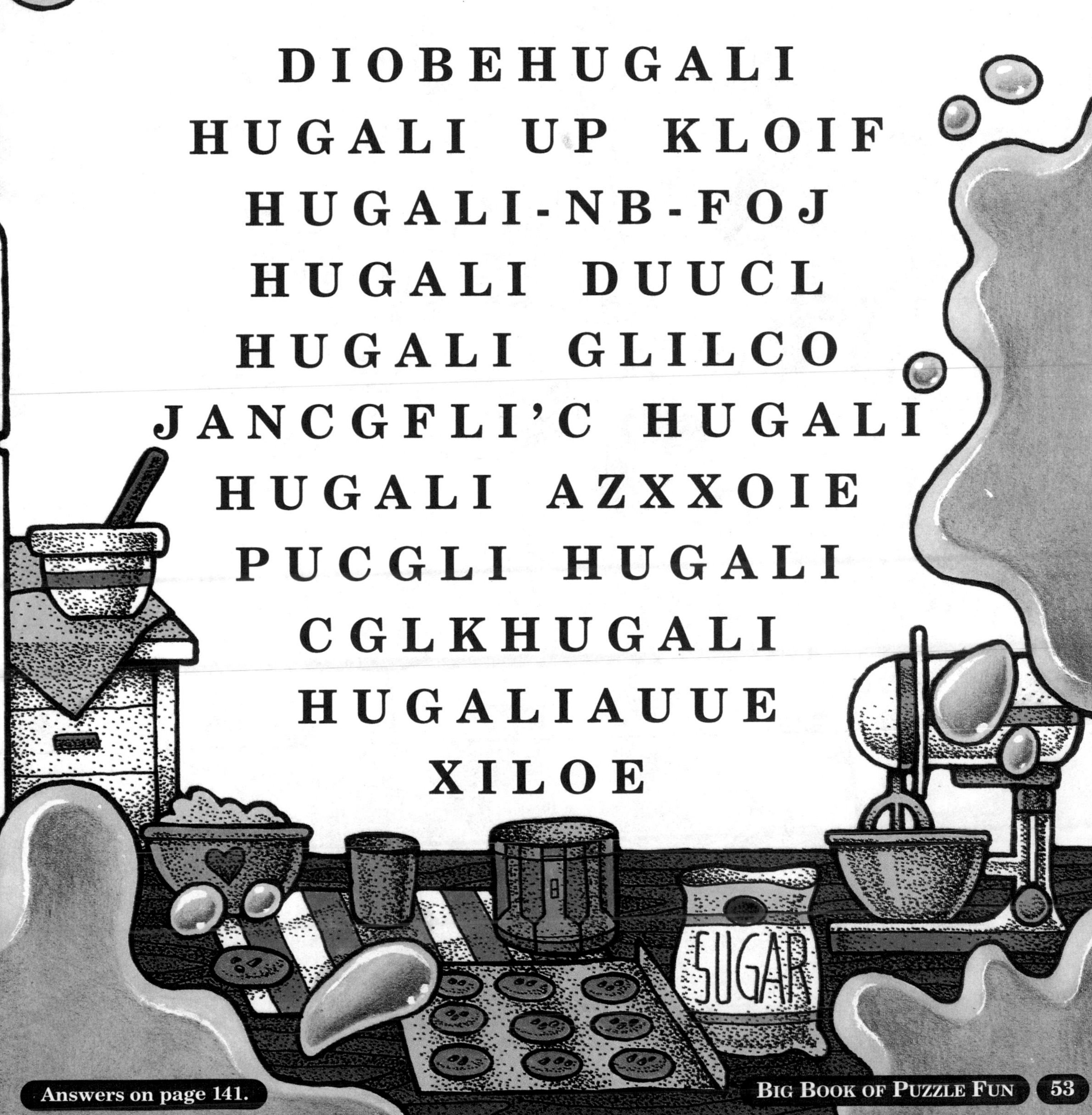

DIOBEHUGALI

HUGALI UP KLOIF

HUGALI-NB-FOJ

HUGALI DUUCL

HUGALI GLILCO

JANCGFLI'C HUGALI

HUGALI AZXXOIE

PUCGLI HUGALI

CGLKHUGALI

HUGALIAUUE

XILOE

Answers on page 141.

THE AGONY OF THE FEET
Can you show who's looking for which shoes?
?
7
1

Answers on page 141.

That's Shoe Business

Can you fit all these shoe words into the right boxes? Use the number of letters in each word as clues to see where they belong. Some words may go together in different ways, but all the words can fit in only one unique design. It may help to cross each word off the list when you use it.

4 Letters
BOOT
CLOG
PUMP
SKIS

5 Letters
CLEAT
FLATS

6 Letters
BOOTIE
BROGAN
WADERS

7 Letters
HIGH TOP
LOAFERS
SANDALS
SNEAKER

8 Letters
FLIP-FLOP
GALOSHES
MOCCASIN
SLIPPERS
TOE SHOES

9 Letters
HIGH HEELS
ICE SKATES

10 Letters
HORSESHOES

12 Letters
ROLLER SKATES

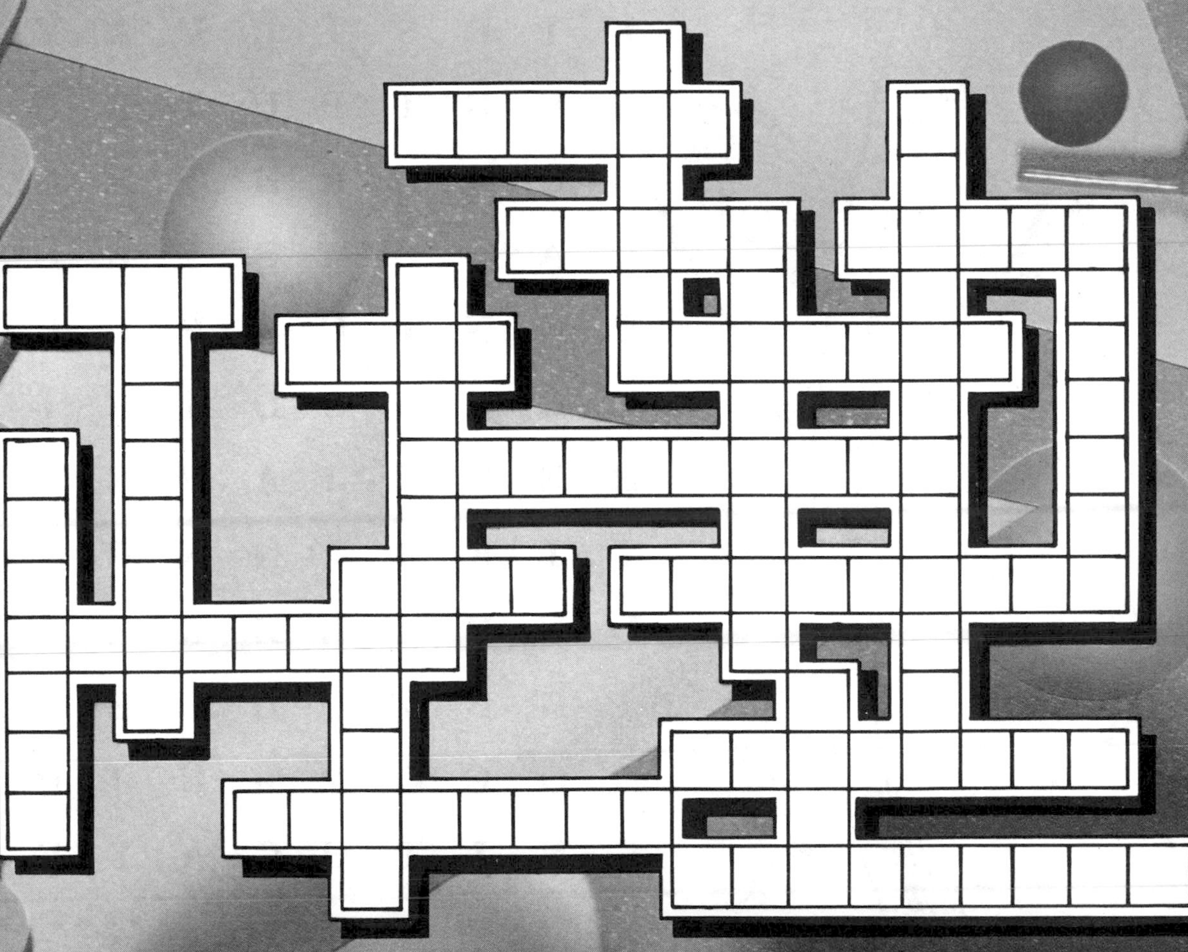

The correct fit is shown on page 141.

Go for the Gold

You'll win first prize if you can find all the Olympic events hidden in the grid below. The events are from both the summer and winter games. Look up, down, across, backward, and diagonally. As you find each word, circle it and then cross it off the list.

Good luck as you compete for the gold.

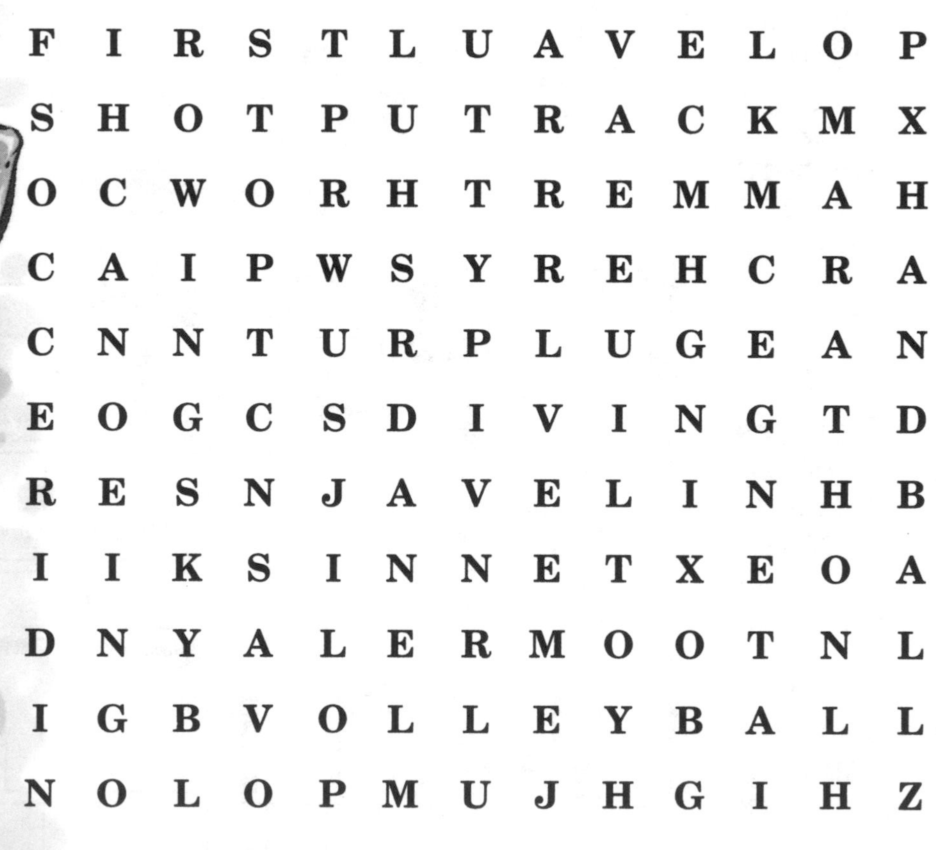

Archery	Hammer throw	Pole vault	Ski
Boxing	Handball	Polo (water)	Soccer
Canoeing	High jump	Relay	Tennis
Discus	Hockey	Riding	Track
Diving	Javelin	Rowing	Volleyball
Gymnastics	Luge	Run	Yachting
	Marathon	Shot put	

F	I	R	S	T	L	U	A	V	E	L	O	P
S	H	O	T	P	U	T	R	A	C	K	M	X
O	C	W	O	R	H	T	R	E	M	M	A	H
C	A	I	P	W	S	Y	R	E	H	C	R	A
C	N	N	T	U	R	P	L	U	G	E	A	N
E	O	G	C	S	D	I	V	I	N	G	T	D
R	E	S	N	J	A	V	E	L	I	N	H	B
I	I	K	S	I	N	N	E	T	X	E	O	A
D	N	Y	A	L	E	R	M	O	O	T	N	L
I	G	B	V	O	L	L	E	Y	B	A	L	L
N	O	L	O	P	M	U	J	H	G	I	H	Z
G	N	I	T	H	C	A	Y	E	K	C	O	H

Leap to page 141 for the answer.

Going for the Hold

These Olympic athletes are all competing in different events, each in quest of a gold medal. But they got so excited they forgot their pieces of equipment. From their positions, try to match the athletes with what they should be holding.

Answers on page 141.

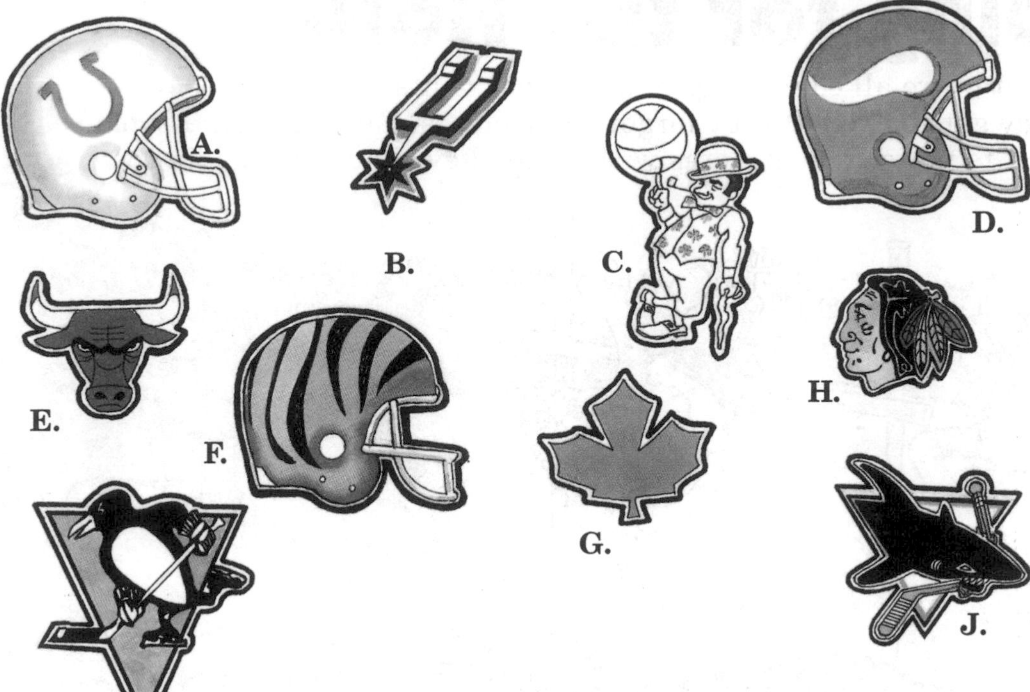

Headgear

Can you fill in the name of each team whose helmet or emblem is shown here?

A. ____________________

B. ____________________

C. ____________________

D. ____________________

E. ____________________

F. ____________________

G. ____________________

H. ____________________

I. ____________________

J. ____________________

What a Dive!

The Olympic Diving Competition was winding down. Bellywhop Willie, Jackknife Jane, Cannonball Clem, and Backflip Flo were locked in a head-over-heels struggle for the gold. They all tried a triple-reverse, double-half-dual-axel gainer with a 98.3% degree of difficulty. Their scores were a perfect 10, 9.6, 8.7, and 4.3. Use the clues below to determine which diver got what medal and who finished out in the cold.

Use the chart to keep track of your answers. Put an "X" in each box that can't be true, and an "O" in the boxes where the information matches.

	Gold 10.0	Silver 9.6	Bronze 8.7	Forget it! 4.3
Bellywhop Willie				
Jackknife Jane				
Cannonball Clem				
Backflip Flo				

1. The Yugoslavian judge took points off because Jane did a double-reverse, triple gainer instead of a triple-reverse, double gainer. She did not win a bronze medal.

2. Backflip Flo flopped when she should have flipped, and that did not please either the French or Brazilian judges. She finished one place behind Jane.

3. Bellywhop Willie did not do as well as Clem.

Answers on page 141.

Bumbling Bowlers

The Puzzle Pals are at the bowling alley. But they don't seem to be having much luck. Can you score a few strikes by finding all the unusual things in this scene?

Illustrated by Leslie Harris

Hoop-Hoop-Hooray

One basketball team is celebrating a narrow victory over its opponent. By looking at the teams' statistics, can you tell which team won?

FG = 2-point field goal
FT = 1-point free throw

Barkley Bears

Player	*FG*	*FT*
M. Stretch	5	3
T. Reach	7	4
U. Shoot	6	2
I. Throw	4	2
L. Pass	3	3
R.E. Bound	3	1
N.O. Fouls	2	3

Tiffany Tigers

Player	*FG*	*FT*
T. Net	4	3
J. Dunk	5	4
L.A. Upp	6	0
G.O. Team	7	5
I. Catch	3	0
H.I. Center	6	5
M. Guard	0	2

Final Scores: ________ ________

Shoot for the answer on page 141.

Build-a-Bike Maze

Danny and Mr. Fix-it want to build a bicycle, but the parts they need are scattered all around the junkyard. Help Danny and Mr. Fix-it by picking up all the bicycle parts on Danny's list as you travel along the only path through the junkyard.

Answers on page 141.

Casey at the Bat

"Casey at the Bat" is such a famous poem that it's even in the Baseball Hall of Fame in Cooperstown, NY. But it never would have gotten there if they saw what happened to this excerpted version. In different parts of the poem, we put the wrong words in capital letters. Find the correct words in the batter's box below and write them into the spaces next to the sentences where they belong.

The outlook wasn't brilliant for the Mudville ELEVEN that day, _________

The score stood four to two, with but one inning more to EAT, _________

And so, when Cooney died at first, and Barrows did the same,

A sickly silence fell upon the patrons of the DINER. _________

• • •

Then from the gladdened multitude went up a joyous CLOUD, _________

It bounded from the mountain-top, and rattled in the dell,

It struck upon the hillside, and recoiled upon the flat,

For Casey, mighty Casey, was advancing to the HOTEL. _________

• • •

There was ease in Casey's manner as he stepped into his PANTS, _________

There was pride in Casey's bearing, and a WART on Casey's face, _________

And when, responding to the cheers, he lightly ATE his hat, _________

No stranger in the crowd could doubt 'twas Casey at the bat.

The sneer is gone from Casey's lips, his EARS are clenched in hate, _________

He pounds with cruel violence his LOLLIPOP upon the plate, _________

And now the pitcher holds the SOAP and now he lets it go, _________

And now the air is shattered by the force of Casey's blow.

• • •

Oh!, somewhere in this favored land the NOSE is shining bright, _________

The FROG is playing somewhere, and somewhere hearts are light, _________

And somewhere men are laughing, and somewhere children shout,

But there is no joy in Mudville—Mighty Casey has struck OIL. _________

BATTER'S BOX

Ball	Nine	Play
Band	Out	Smile
Bat	Place	Sun
Doffed	Plate	Teeth
Game		Yell

Answers on page 141.

Mighty Casey

In this large picture of Casey, find the mouse, fork, pencil, hamburger, ant, toothbrush, mushroom, squirrel, bird, comb, rabbit, wristwatch, snake, man-in-the-moon, mallet, fish, accordion, and the heads of a goat and an alligator.

Illustrated by Kit Wray

Let's Play!

Games are a terrific way to have fun.
Can you name a game to go with each piece of equipment shown?

Home Run Derby

Wayne, Pepe, Hans, and Jennifer each play on a team in Mudville's Little Baseball League. Using the clues below, figure out who played in the most games and who got the most home runs.

1. Wayne played in seven games and got four home runs.
2. Pepe played in two more games than Wayne, but he got one less home run.
3. Hans played in more games than Wayne but in fewer games than Pepe. He got half as many home runs as Jennifer.
4. Jennifer played in half as many games as Hans, and she got two home runs in each game.

Answers on page 141.

Song of the Sea

See if you can solve this fishy code to come up with the name of Monstro's favorite song.

 A

 B

 C

 D

E

 F

 G

H

 I

 J

 K

 L

 M

 N

 O

 P

Q

 R

 S

 T

U

 V

W

 X

 Y

 Z

Answers on page 141.

How many triangles are in this star?

Answer is on page 34.

Bubble Trouble

Each of these floating bubbles contains the name of something that is round. Before the bubbles burst, can you figure out what round thing is inside each one?

Harvest Signs

Rebus Rita has been doing more planting. See if you can read each sign to figure out what's in her garden.

Answers on page 141-142.

Grandpa's Tall Tales

While fishing, Grandpa told some tall tales. Can you spot the mistakes in each of Grandpa's stories?

There we were, my friend Dave and I, sitting in the boat up on Lake Manatee. It had been a really slow morning. The bass were so small we kept throwing them back. I was nearly bored to sleep when suddenly I felt a nibble. The nibble became a yank. One minute I was daydreaming, the next I was slamming into Dave, way up at the prow. If he hadn't grabbed my arm, I'd have gone right into the water. We both struggled with the rod, trying to reel in the whopper. That was one furious fish! No way was it going to let us catch it. It got close enough for me to get a glimpse. It was the biggest, meanest, ugliest catfish you'd ever want to see. What a monster! It must have sensed we were getting tired, because it gave a mighty tug. Instead of jerking me, it jerked the whole boat. The beast was towing us! Dave said that anything that determined to live deserved to be free. So he cut the line. The last I saw of that fish was his huge fin gliding through the water out toward the center of the lake.

Now here's another great story. One time, Grandma Amanda and I were playing hide-and-seek in my dad's old barn. I hid behind a butter churn stored in one corner.

Amanda looked everywhere for me, but all she could find was lots of silky spider webs.

"I'm over here," I hollered to her. "You couldn't find me, but look what I found."

And I held out three copper pennies.

"How old are they?" Amanda asked.

"I can't tell. The dates are rusty. Let's go and see if we can clean them up."

Then we ran off to get some soap and water.

These stories are cleared up on page 142.

Flight of the Honeybees

Lead the bees back to the hive so they can begin making honey.

Illustrated by Judith Hunt

Start

Finish

Buzz over to the answer on page 142.

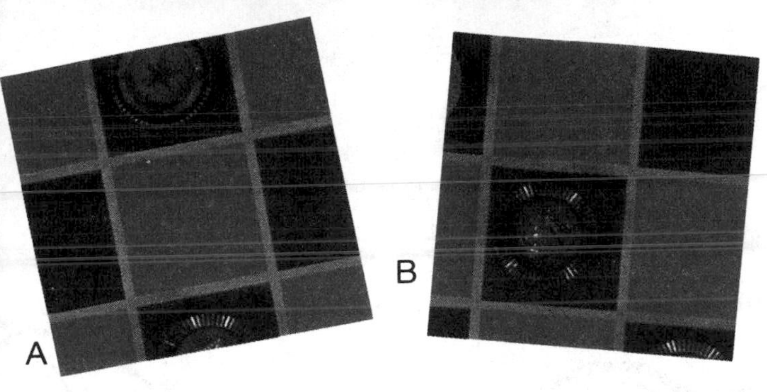

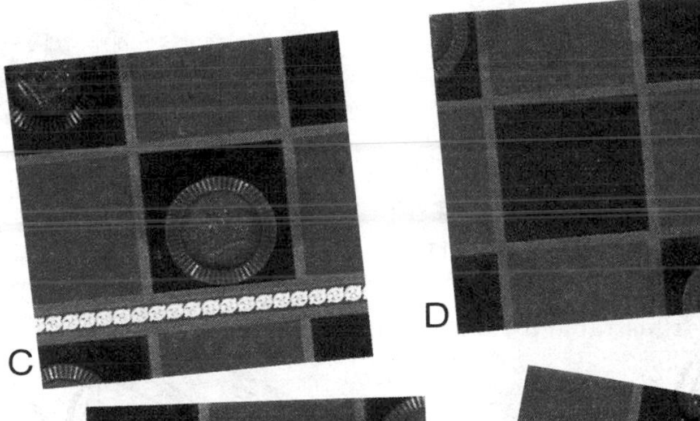

Checkers Champ

Be the checkers champ by figuring out which of the puzzle pieces above are the missing squares from the checkerboard below.

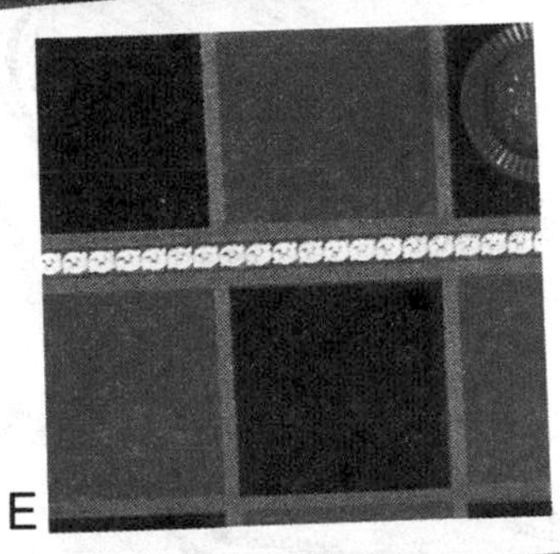

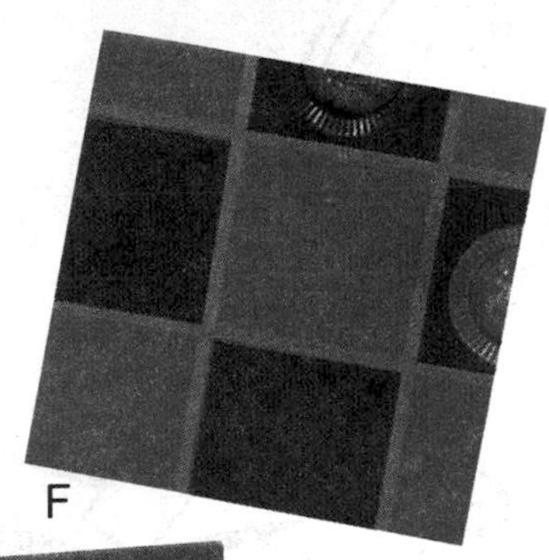

1

2

3

Answers on page 142.

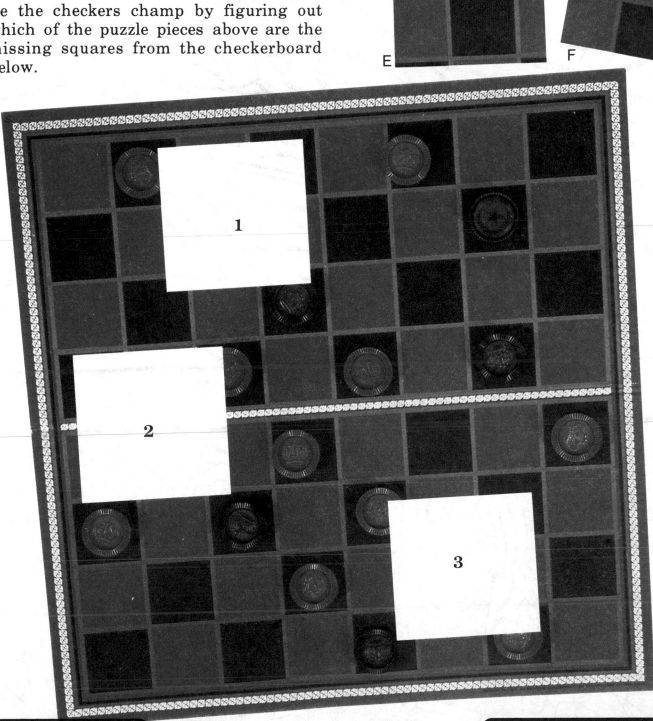

Reel Confusion

The theater is packed for the debut of the famous Canned Film Festival. Four feature movies have been entered for the showing, but the projectionists got the films mixed up and the crowd is getting restless. The temperamental Swedish film queen, Rula Thumb, has already walked out. See if you can follow the four reels of film to their proper projectors.

Illustrated by Corbin Hillam

A B C D

1 2 3 4

The flicks are fixed on page 142.

Here's our first famous movie scene! Dorothy and her friends won't be allowed into Emerald City until they can find all the hidden objects. Scan this large picture to find Dorothy's ruby slipper, her basket, Toto's bone, Tin Woodsman's oil can, his axe, his heart, Glinda's wand, the Wicked Witch's head, her broom, and a butterfly.

Illustrated by Steve Smallwood

Film Fun

During intermission, Linc came up with a code using items in the theater. Use the key below to find the titles of two of Missing Linc's favorite films.

A B C D E F G H I J K L M

N O P Q R S T U V W X Y Z

THE END

Illustrated by Chris Reed

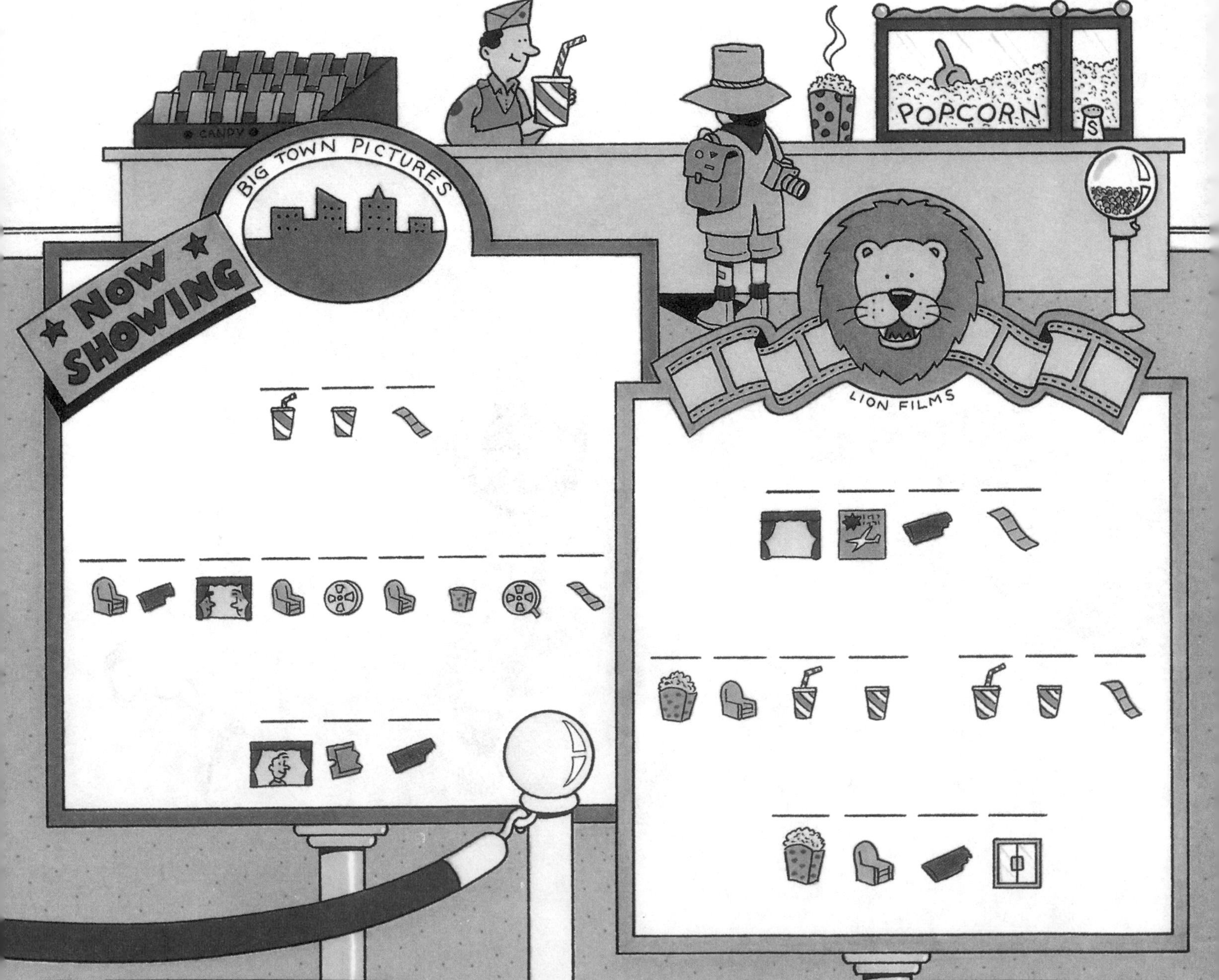

POPCORN

BIG TOWN PICTURES

NOW SHOWING

LION FILMS

Titles roll on page 142

Creature Feature

A crazy collection of critters has been invited for their own private screening of *Animal House*. To find out the answer to the riddle, look at the number and letter below each space. The letter stands for the row, and the number stands for the seat in which each creature is sitting. When you've found the seat, identify the animal sitting in it, and place the first letter of that animal's name over the space. For example, seat B5 has an alligator sitting in it, so an "A" goes over the first space.

What kind of tryout do they give for horror movies?

___   ___ ___ ___ ___ ___ ___   ___ ___ ___ ___

B5 • B3 C2 E5 A2 B5 B1 • D1 A4 D5 C4

Illustrated by Judith Hunt

Answers on page 142.

POP THE QUESTION

It's time to pop the question. For Father's Day, we've written the clues for ten famous "pops." Fill in the missing spaces. Then answer the question at the bottom by filling in letters to match each number.

1. Movie Snack: 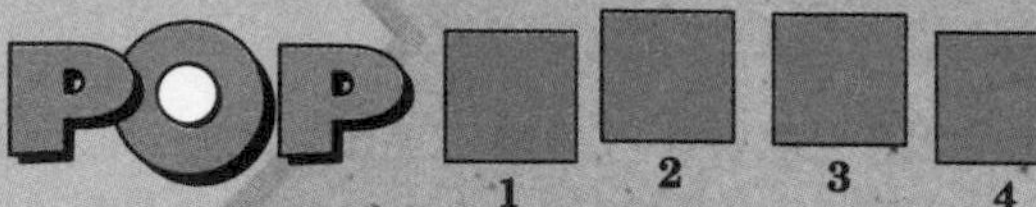

2. Head of the Roman Catholic Church: 

3. A kind of tree: 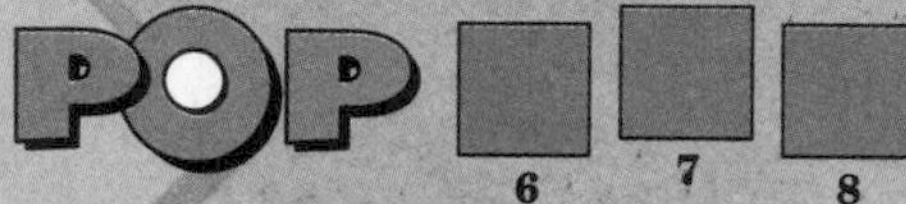

4. A kind of fabric: 

5. A type of dark seed that goes on bagels and cakes: 

6. The number of people who live in one place: 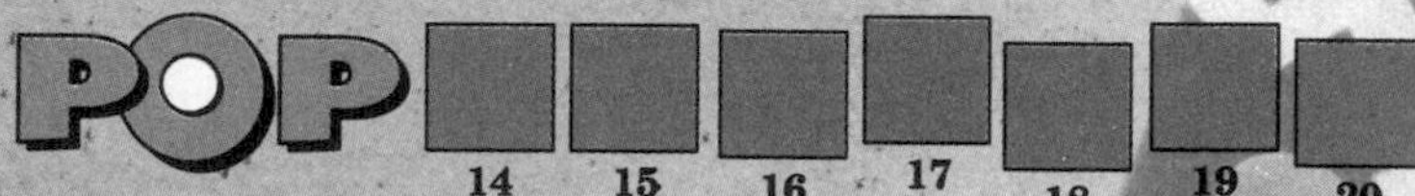

7. Well liked: 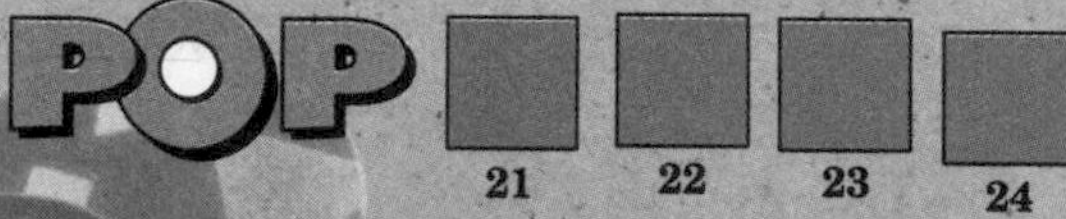

8. Cartoon sailor: 

9. Candy on a stick: 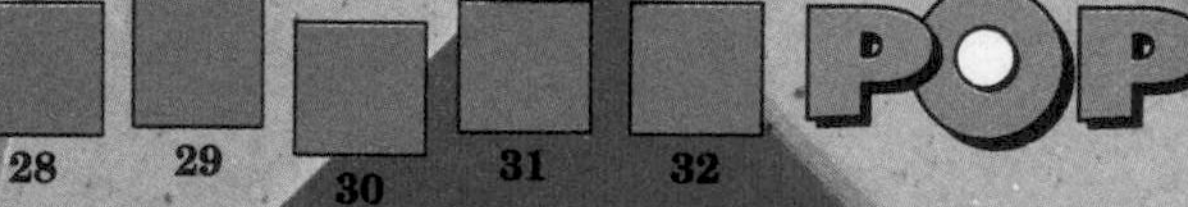

10. Popcorn-makers: 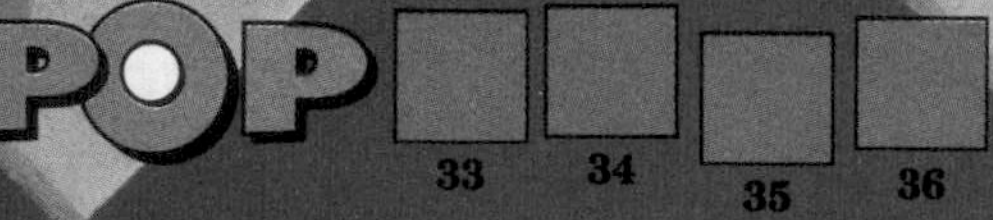

What kind of bikes do fathers ride?

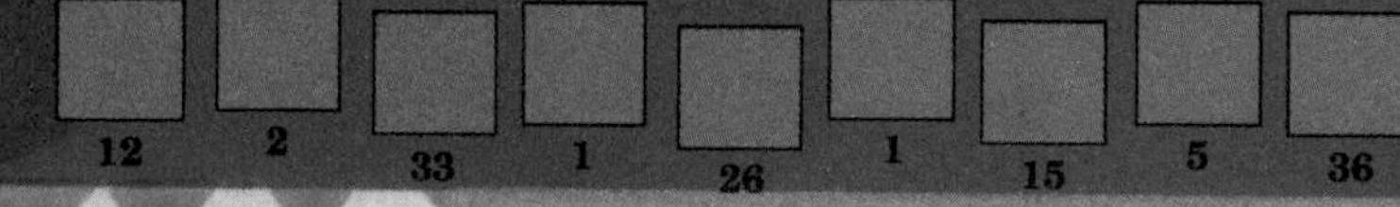

Answers on page 142.

FOR GOODNESS SNAKES

This explorer is going to have to sift through all those snakes if he wants to find the goblet, bagel, wristwatch, bow tie, cornucopia horn, fish, golf ball, necktie, iron, fishhook, boomerang, spoon, heart, pear, spatula, and a slice of pie.

Going Fourth

Unscramble each word to discover the names of the first 13 colonies that became the original United States in 1776.

Once you've got all the colonies signed up, look for the letters in the different colored boxes. Copy those letters in order into the boxes below to receive an important message for the Fourth of July.

1. ROHED NAILSD
2. ERAGOGI
3. YESPLAINVANN
4. WEN HAPIHERMS
5. WNE KROY
6. GRINIAVI
7. WEN YESJER
8. CUTECITONNC
9. THORN LIONCARA
10. WEEDLARA
11. CHUMSTSATSEAS
12. ARMYLAND
13. SHOUT OARCLINA

(5)

(8)

!(7)

Answers on page 142.

Crosspatch

To read this riddle, hold the book at eye level, and look across the page.

To read the answer, turn the page sideways, and look across it again.

Mistake at the Museum

When Katie saw this painting in the museum, she noticed something peculiar about it. The museum guide said the painting was done when Abraham Lincoln was President, but Katie said it couldn't have been painted until years later. Can you find at least five things in the painting that prove Katie is correct?

★★

Lincoln Logic

One of the flags shown here was used during Lincoln's presidency. To figure out which one, use the clues below.

1. South Dakota became the 40th state in 1889.
2. The number of stars on each flag shown here stands for the number of states that belonged to the union when that flag was in use.
3. Lincoln was president from 1861 to 1865.
4. Rhode Island became the 13th state in 1790, and fifty-five years later the union had fifteen more states.

Answers on page 142.

JUMPIN' GEOGRAPHY!

The names of some towns with their state names actually make humorous phrases. Here are six cartoons of some funny town and state names we found. Match each one with the name from the list below that it seems to describe. Then look at maps to see how many other funny town and state combinations you can find.

Tow, Texas
Pinch, West Virginia
Roll, Arizona
Load, Kentucky
Chase, Maryland
Snowball, Arkansas

1.

2.

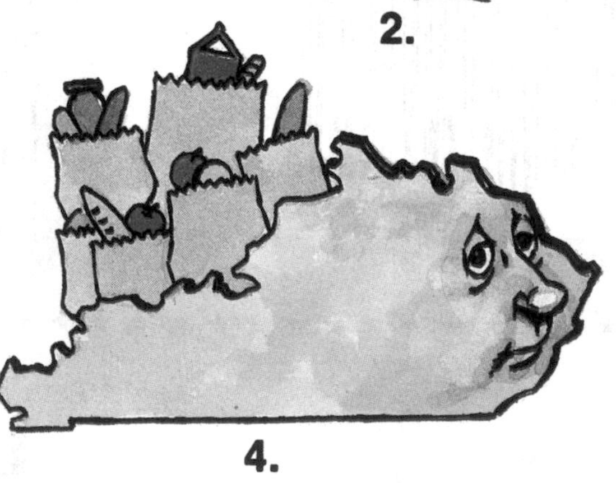

Illustrated by Marc Nadel

Answers on page 142.

Capital Crossword

Here's a capital idea. It's your big chance to show how well you know your capitals. For each state given as a clue, fill in the grid with the capital that goes with it. Don't forget to use **CAPITAL** letters.

Answers on page 142.

LOST AT "C"
Check your compass to completely chart these "C's" and conclude the correct calculation of how many things in this picture commence with the letter "C."
CAB
Illustrated by Tim Ellis

Time Find

Each of these clocks shows a specific time during the countdown for the launch of the latest mission to Saturn. These times were supposed to have been translated into the standard digital readouts below. But a bug got into the computer, causing an overflow of numbers. Can you help the computer find each time so that the engineers can carry out their safety check? Look up, down, across, backward, or diagonally to find each time.

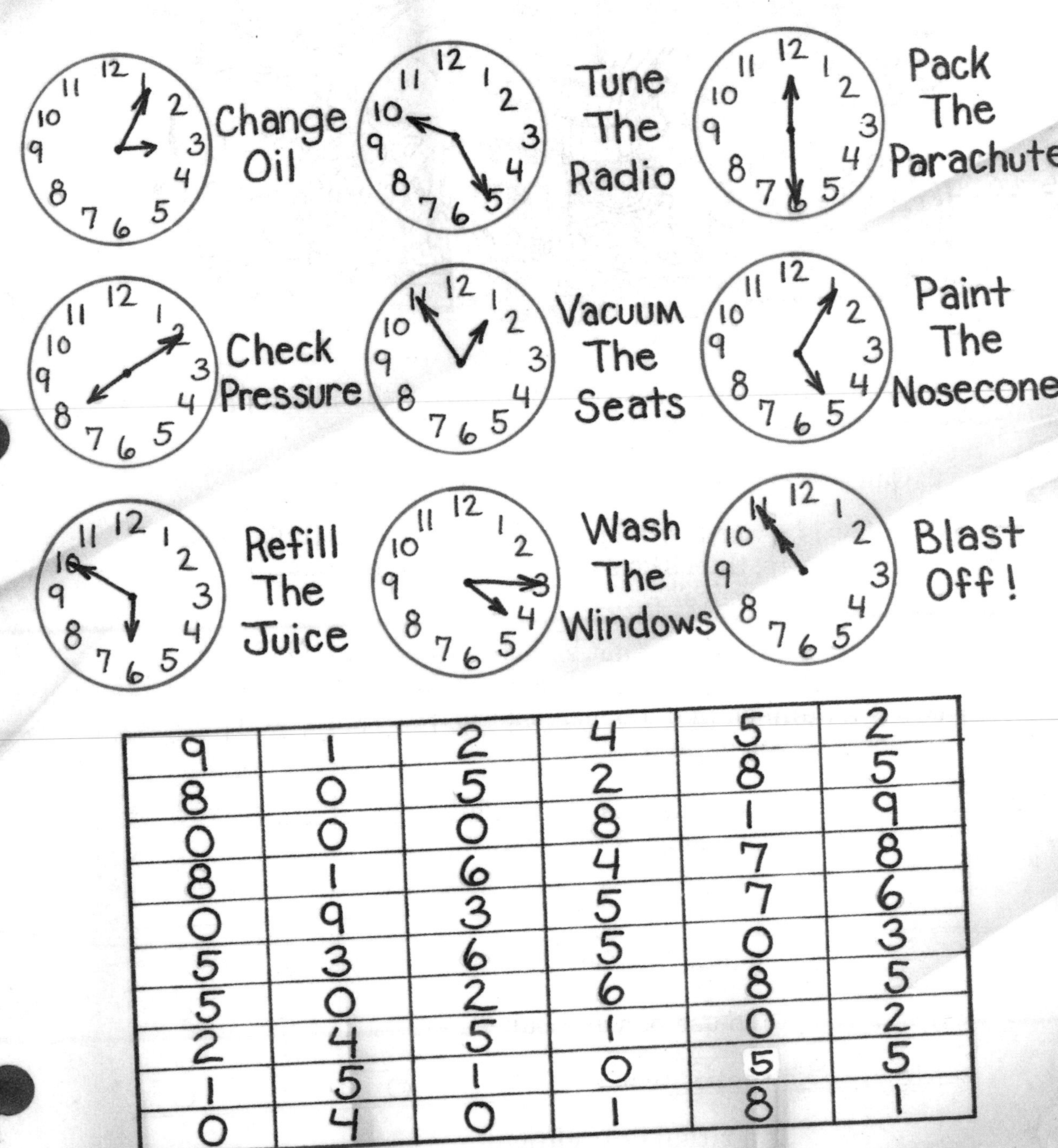

9	1	2	4	5	2
8	0	5	2	8	5
0	0	0	8	1	9
8	1	6	4	7	8
0	9	3	5	7	6
5	3	6	5	0	3
5	0	2	6	8	5
2	4	5	1	0	2
1	5	1	0	5	5
0	4	0	1	8	1

Answers on page 142.

Word Works

1. What three-letter verb can be changed to its own past tense by moving the first letter to the end?
2. Can you spell CANDY using just two letters?
3. Pillow is a word with one letter pair, the l's. Toffee has two letter pairs, the f's and the e's. Can you name a word that has three letter pairs?

Homonyms are words that have the same sound but very different meanings. For example, to is a directional word, while two is a number, and too means also. See if you can tell which homonyms belong in the blanks below.

4. __________ means this place, while __________ means sound is registering in your ear.
5. __________: to cry or scream

   __________: not a fish, but the world's largest mammal
6. __________: to use pen and paper

   __________: opposite of left

   __________: a ritual or tradition

Answers on page 142.

Double-Use W's

There are two puzzles on this page. First, a whole wagonload of words which begin with W are pictured here. Word wizards will find at least 23 "W" words.

Next there are four sets of words that have double uses and may sound the same. For example, the boy is whistling a note, and the girl at the table is writing a note. Can you find the other double-use pairs?

Illustrated by Charles Jordan

Just for Decoration

How many cubes can you see in this pattern? In this puzzle, cubes look like three-sided squares.

Starry Night

How quickly can you spot if there are more white stars or more dark stars in the sky?

The answers are hanging on page 142.

Bungling Builders

How many unusual things can you find happening in this picture?

Which Way to Adventure?

Each of these characters had many exciting adventures. Match each one with the scene where some of the adventures took place and with the book that tells the story.

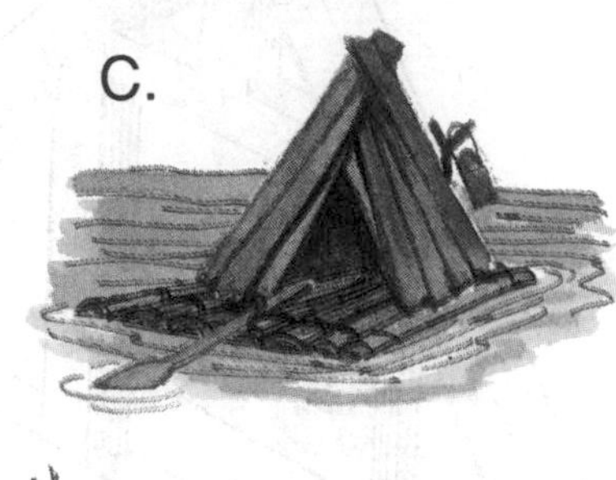

Illustrated by Anni Matsick

The answers are told on page 142.

Whose Birthday?

The animals are all celebrating someone's eighth birthday. Figure out who the birthday animal is by using the clues below. Which animal is the oldest?

1. The birthday critter is not Lion.
2. Baboon is three years older than Turtle.
3. Turtle is the same age as Lion.
4. Lion is two years older than Raccoon.
5. Raccoon is two years older than Duck.
6. Duck and Elephant are each four years old.

PART 1

Logical Lee is packing for camp, but he wants to take EVERYTHING he owns. Unfortunately, all of it won't fit in the car. His mother told him to take one thing beginning with each letter of the alphabet (A to Z). After laying everything out, Lee will take a long look and then leave the room. Whatever he remembers, he'll bring. See if you can help Logical Lee by looking at this picture for 30 seconds. Then turn to the next page and write down everything you can remember from A-Z, without turning back to this picture. Logical Lee is depending on you!

You Can Take It With You

PART 2

OK, Logical Lee is counting on you to remember as many things as you can so he can bring them to camp. List all of his belongings from "A to Z." Don't look back until you're done!

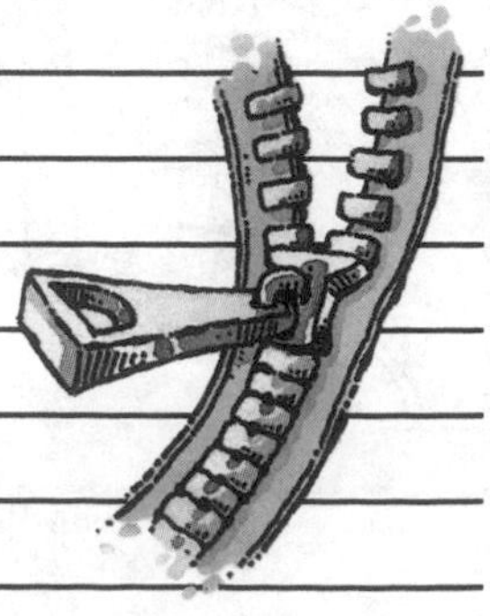

Wheel Fun

The Ferris wheel is coming to a stop, but all the Puzzle Pals can't get off at the same time. Going clockwise, the man will stop the wheel at every third car. If he starts with Rita in car 2, and follows the pattern all the way through, which of the Pals will be the last one off the wheel?

Illustrated by Tom Powers

Answer on page 142.

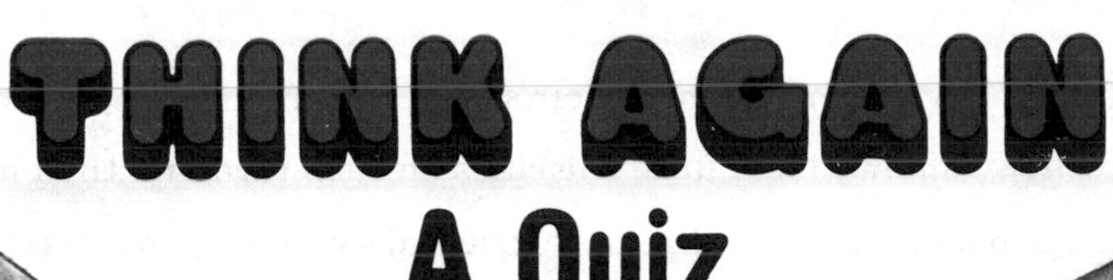

THINK AGAIN
A Quiz

1. If you take two apples from a basket of five apples, how many do you have?

2. A farmer had twelve sheep. All but eight of them ran away. How many sheep did he have left?

3. How many 15-cent postcards are there in two dozen?

4. How many gumdrops can you place in an empty quart jar?

5. How far can a deer run into the forest?

6. How much dirt is there in a hole two feet long, four feet wide, and one foot deep?

7. If a doctor gave you three pills and told you to take one every half-hour, how many hours would go by before the pills were gone?

8. If you had two United States coins totaling thirty cents and one was not a quarter, what would they be?

9. Draw six lines like this: | | | | | |. Now add five more lines to create nine.

10. Which weighs more, a pound of feathers or a pound of lead?

11. A man has seven black socks and six white socks in his drawer. Without looking, he reached into the drawer to get a pair of socks. What is the smallest number of socks he could take to be sure that he gets a matched pair?

Answers on page 142.

Locker Up!

The Puzzle Pals have been assigned their school lockers, but they need a little help to figure out their combinations. Read the clues on each card and then look around the school to determine each Puzzle Pal's correct combination. Hurry—homeroom starts in five minutes!

LOBBY

PRIN
OFFI

NURSES OFFICE
Back at 10

37

ELLIS

Max

1. Look at the back of the football player's T-shirt.
2. Count the number of kids carrying lunch boxes.
3. Count the number of books Lee is holding.

___ (L) ___ (R) ___ (L)

Millie

1. Look for the room number of Ms. Toivenon's class.
2. Count the buttons on the shirt of the principal, Mr. Campbell.
3. Look at the number the custodian is sweeping up.

___ (L) ___ (R) ___ (L)

4
CAFETERIA
GIRLS LOCKER ROOM
11 MS. Toivenon
Roy
1. Check the top of the fire bell.
2. Count the dots on Dotty's outfit.
3. Look where the small hand of the clock is pointing.
(L) (R) (L)
Lee
1. Check the time the note says the nurse will return.
2. Count how many letters are in the word "cafeteria."
3. Count how many girls are lined up outside Ms. Leopold's locker room.
(L) (R) (L)
Dotty
1. Count how many people are standing in the lobby.
2. Count the crayons on Roy's bandolier.
3. Count the number of kids in the hallway who are wearing sneakers.
(L) (R) (L)

Unlock the answer on page 142.

BIG GAME HUNT

Linc is a big football fan who goes to every home game. Can you hunt for him at this one? Also hunt for a sailor, a scarecrow, and a skunk.

Illustrated by Frank Bolle

The Audition Decision

Auditions for the school play, "Macbeth Meets the Abominable Snowman," were held in the school auditorium. Roy, Lee, Max, and Millie were all trying for different roles: Macbeth, the Snowman, the Scarecrow (which they borrowed from another story), and a tree. Macbeth was the lead. The Snowman had no lines but got to grunt a lot and was the second biggest part. The Scarecrow got to do a neat song-and-dance bit in the second act, and the tree just stood there. Use the clues below to determine what Pal got which part.

	Macbeth	Abominable Snowman	Scarecrow	Tree
Roy				
Lee				
Max				
Millie				

1. Roy did a tap dance routine, but the director did not have in mind an Abominable Snowman who could tap dance.

2. Millie sang "New York, New York," but blew the line "These vagabond shoes." She did not get the lead role.

3. Max did a rap version of Hamlet's famed soliloquy, "To Be or Not to Be." He did not get as big a part as Millie.

4. Lee belted out a powerful rendition of "Old Man River." He got the singing part.

REF-A-REASON

In a preseason demonstration, these four teams all started on the fifty-yard line, but they each made a few mistakes. Add up the penalty yardage to see which team had to go all the way back to the end zone.

offsides • illegal procedure • illegal motion • delay of game • clipping • holding

5 yds. • 5yds. • 5yds. • 5yds. • 10yds. • 10yds.

Answers on page 142.

Library Check-Out

Check out this library to find all the hidden books so the librarian can put them back inside on the shelves.

The Number Encumber

This math class is tough. It's only the first day and already there's a code to crack. First, read the descriptions and figure out what number represents each letter. Next, answer the riddle by placing the correct letters into the spaces that match the numbers below it. For example, B = 8+7, which is 15. So if there's a space marked 15, you should put in a B.

A = number of bones in an adult human being

B = 8 + 7

C = 57 - 19

D = 55 ÷ 11

E = number of continents

F = James Bond's number

G = 99 - 11

H = 0 + 901

I = 62 x 1

J = number of cards in a pinochle deck

K = a baker's dozen

L = number of leaves on a lucky clover

M = number of ears on a person subtracted from the number of toes on one foot

N = number of Tuesdays in an average year

O = 0 ÷ 0

P = number of teeth in an adult person's mouth

Q = Don Mattingly's number

R = number of humps on a Bactrian camel

S = number of nickels in five dollars

T = 1,036 x 1

U = number of holes on top of a whale.

V = number of planets farther from the Sun than Earth

W = 9 x 4

X = number of months with an "R" in them

Y = number of holes on a golf course

Z = number of presidents the U.S. has had as of 1991

What kind of numbers never stay in one place?

____________________________ ,

2 • 0 • 206 • 3 • 62 • 52

____

52 • 1 • 3 • 7 • 2 • 206 • 4 • 100

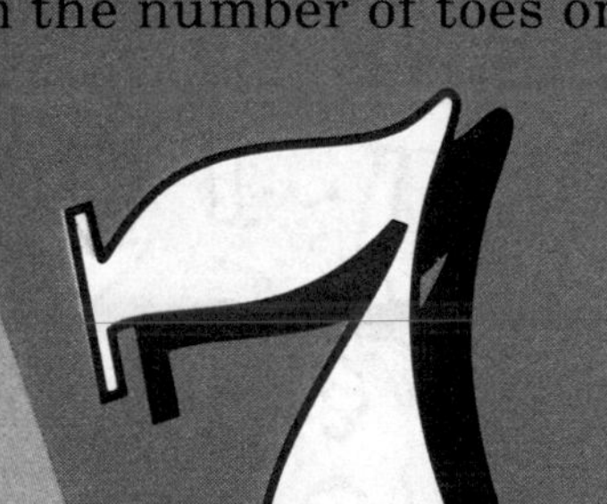

Illustrated by Rob Sepanak

This all adds up on page 142.

Classroom Chaos

This class got a little disorganized on the first day of school. You shouldn't have to be an "A" student to find all the wrong things in this picture.

Answers on page 143.

ARF!
ARF!
ARF!
By matching the blocks scattered around the room with the ones in the castle you'll discover which letters fit into the empty spaces. If you then read the words from bottom to top, you'll learn the answer to the royal riddle.
H
C
K
T
G
T
What does the king use to get his drawbridge to work
O
O
S
T
E
I
O
R
M
A
U
E
R
L

On the Ropes

After making it to the top of the ropes, the Puzzle Pals are having a difficult time getting back down. See if you can lead each Pal down a rope to the correct mat awaiting him or her at the bottom. Hurry, their arms are getting tired!

Answers on page 143.

THE DOG SHOW
A few students brought in their dogs for show-and-tell. See if you can match each dog with its similar-looking owner. Can you also find all the bones these dogs hid before the show began?
MIKE DIETZ

Cash-a-teria

On Fridays, the Puzzle Pals like to buy their lunches in the school cafeteria. By looking at the picture, can you find out who spent the most money on lunch today? Who spent the least? Whose meal cost exactly $3.00?

 The costs are ringing up on page 143.

Illustrated by Leslie Harris

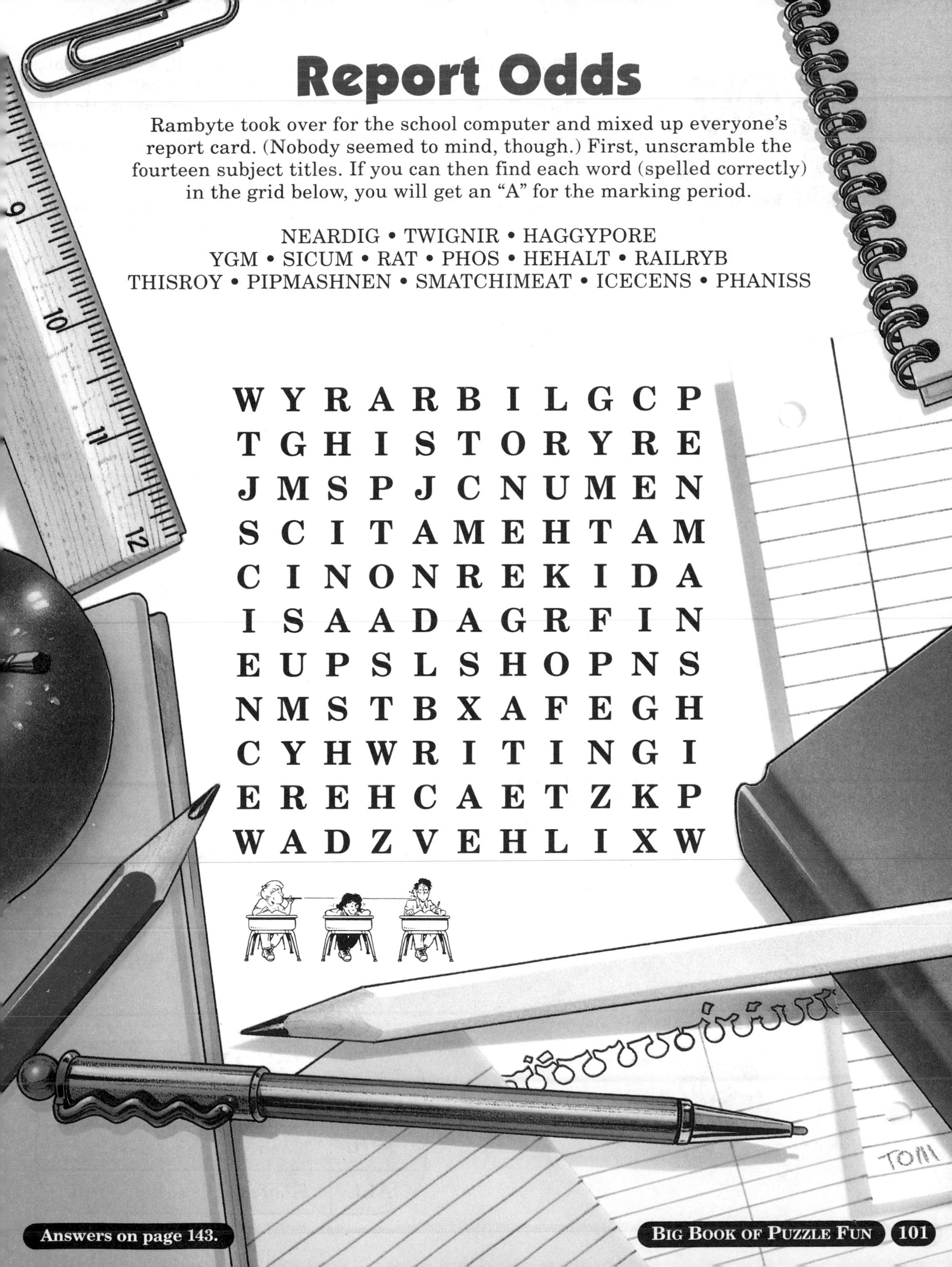

Report Odds

Rambyte took over for the school computer and mixed up everyone's report card. (Nobody seemed to mind, though.) First, unscramble the fourteen subject titles. If you can then find each word (spelled correctly) in the grid below, you will get an "A" for the marking period.

NEARDIG • TWIGNIR • HAGGYPORE
YGM • SICUM • RAT • PHOS • HEHALT • RAILRYB
THISROY • PIPMASHNEN • SMATCHIMEAT • ICECENS • PHANISS

W Y R A R B I L G C P
T G H I S T O R Y R E
J M S P J C N U M E N
S C I T A M E H T A M
C I N O N R E K I D A
I S A A D A G R F I N
E U P S L S H O P N S
N M S T B X A F E G H
C Y H W R I T I N G I
E R E H C A E T Z K P
W A D Z V E H L I X W

Answers on page 143.

PLAY BALL!

A Quiz

1. This player makes his home between second and third base. He is a
   (a) catcher
   (b) shortstop
   (c) coach

2. If the batter makes it to first base after a hit, he belted a
   (a) single
   (b) strike
   (c) foul

3. A fair ball hit high into the air is a
   (a) fly ball
   (b) walk
   (c) grounder

4. The length of a game is measured in
   (a) outs
   (b) years
   (c) innings

5. A fast ball, a knuckle ball, and a curve ball are part of this player's skills. He is a
   (a) catcher
   (b) pitcher
   (c) shortstop

6. When the pitcher allows no runs during a game, it is a
   (a) strikeout
   (b) shutout
   (c) pitchout

7. One way to get an out is for the umpire to call three
   (a) runs
   (b) singles
   (c) strikes

8. The National League and the American League met in 1903 to play the first
   (a) National Cup
   (b) Super Bowl
   (c) World Series

9. When a batter hits the ball out of the playing field, but in fair territory, he has hit a
   (a) strike
   (b) home run
   (c) triple

10. The person who enforces the rules during a baseball game is the
    (a) judge
    (b) manager
    (c) umpire

11. When the pitcher throws the ball outside of the strike zone and the batter doesn't swing, the umpire calls a
    (a) strike
    (b) ball
    (c) run

Illustrated by C. S. Ewing

SCORE	
1-2	Can't get to first base.
3-10	You're on third base.
ALL	Hooray! It's a home run.

Answers on page 143.

Opus Focus

Rebus Rita is having a hard time deciding which instrument she wants to play. "Band" together the picture clues to form the names of the musical instruments Rita is thinking about learning.

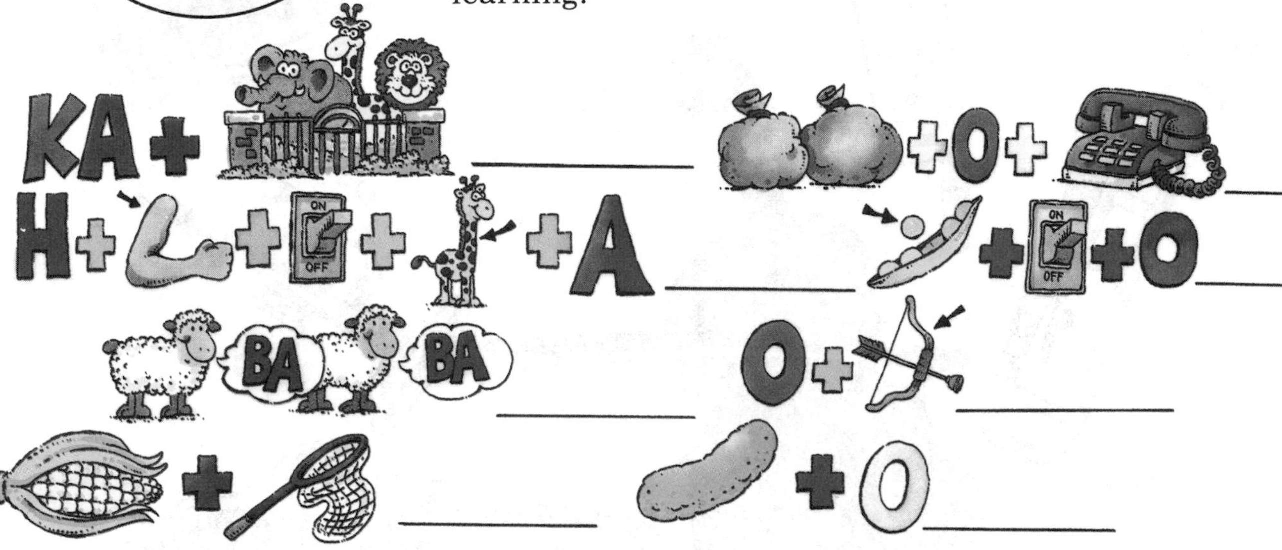

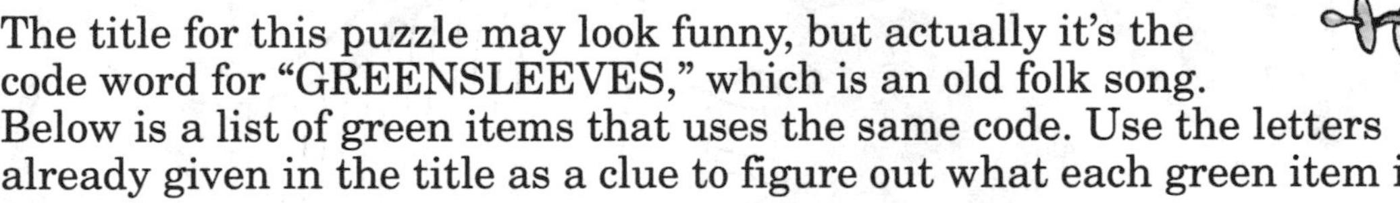

HAPPYZIPPUPZ

The title for this puzzle may look funny, but actually it's the code word for "GREENSLEEVES," which is an old folk song. Below is a list of green items that uses the same code. Use the letters already given in the title as a clue to figure out what each green item is.

1. VIEUPA
2. HE ZOHYLI
3. HALZZ
4. TEIILA JOII
5. KAEHZ
6. REYPQTPB SPIEY
7. PUPAHAPPY FAPPZ
8. IOSP
9. EIOUPZ
10. IPFFWVP
11. HALXPZ
12. SLAFOLYZ
13. HAPPYILYT
14. ZIOSP
15. PYUQ

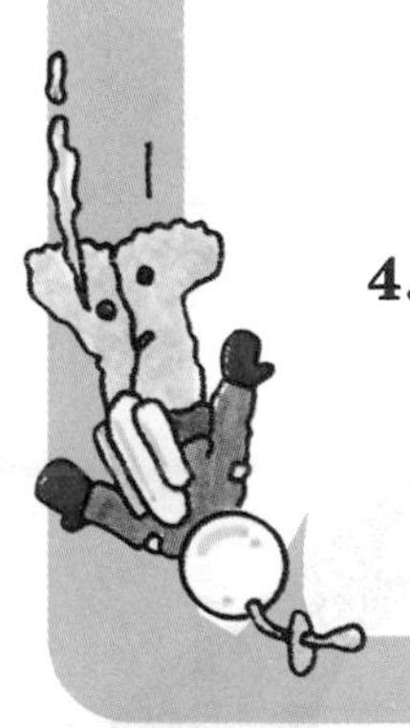

Answers on page 143.

See if you can discover what's unusual about each instrument here.

Illustrated by Craig Tyler

Answers on page 143.

A Puzzle of Note

To make sure the Puzzle Pals learned their scales, the band teacher came up with a puzzle in musical notation. First, look at the scale to determine the letter that goes with each note. Then, see what word has been formed by the musical notes for each clue. Finally, write the words in the proper spaces in the grid.

ACROSS

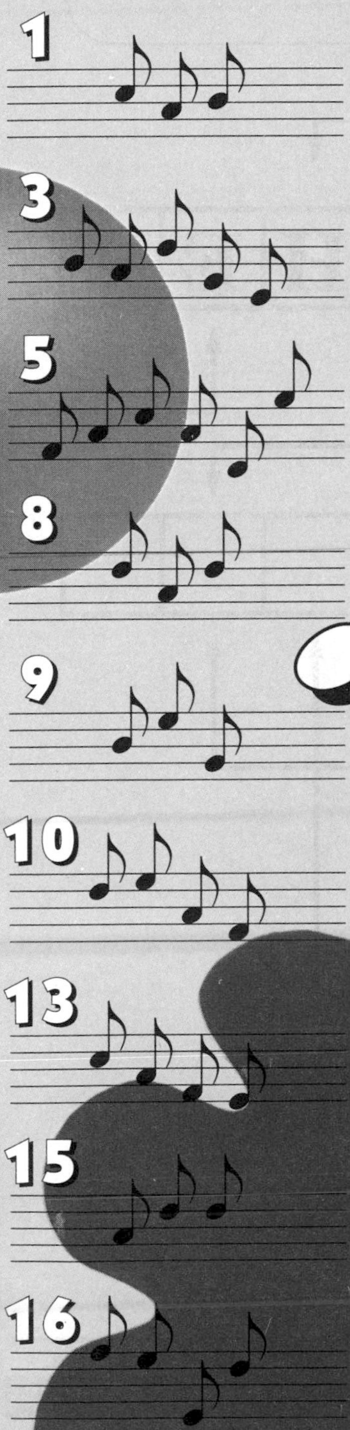

1
3
5
8
9
10
13
15
16

DOWN

2
3
4
6
7
11
12
14

1
2
3
4
5
6
7
8
9
10
11
12
13
14
15
16

SCALE

D E F G A B C D E F G

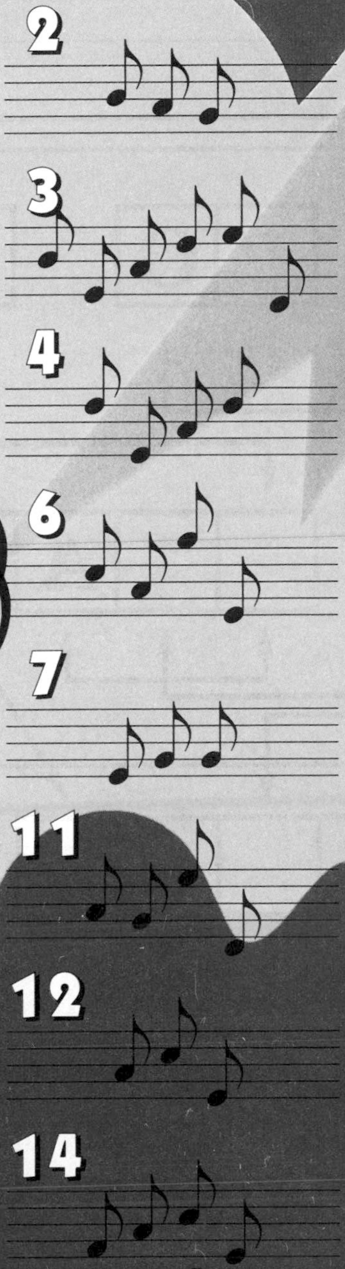

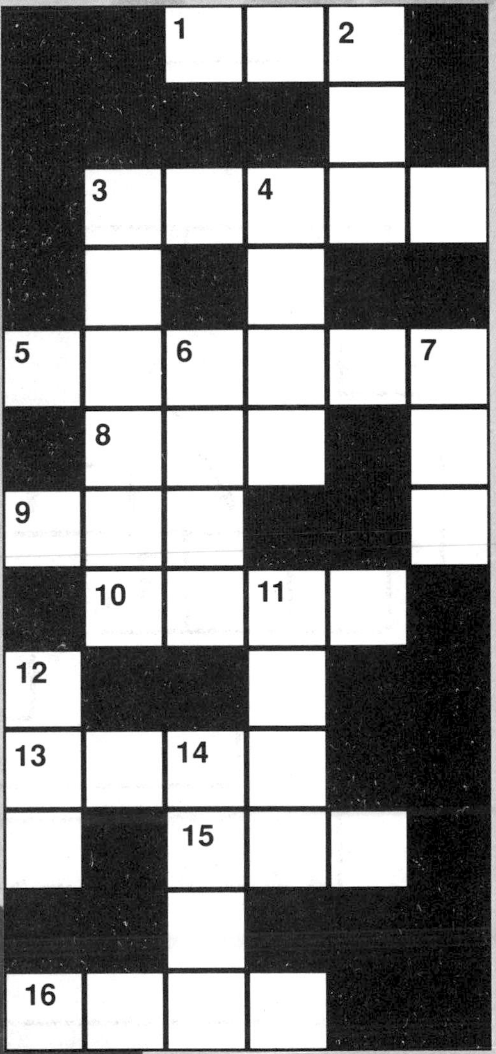

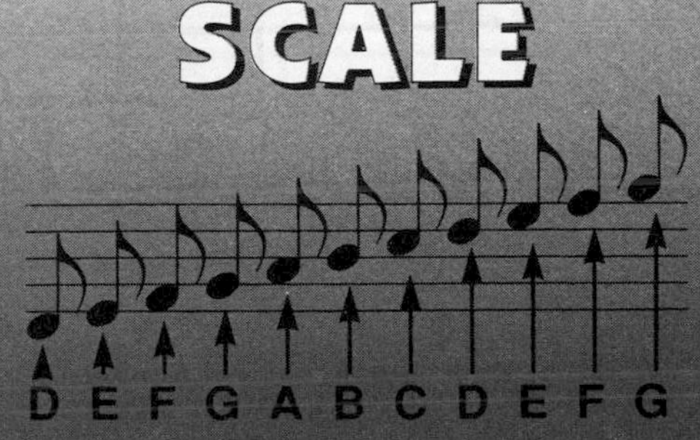

Answers on page 143.

Letter Lines

Though this puzzle looks complicated, it really isn't. Just follow the arrows from box to box, placing the same letter in each connected box. Some starting letters are already given, while some other letters need to be guessed. The more letters you fill in, the easier it gets. When you're finished, you should be able to read a fun riddle.

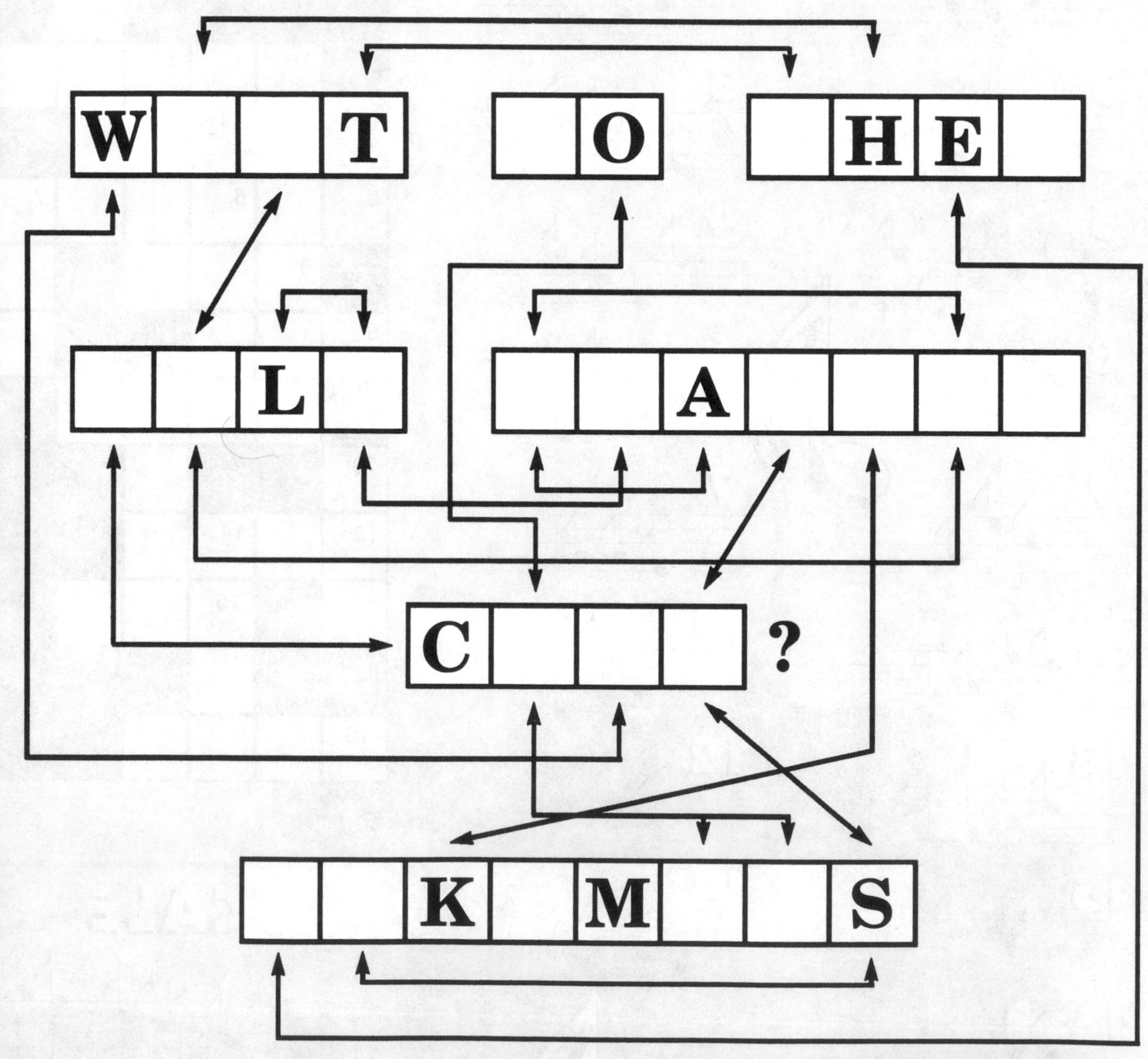

Answers on page 143.

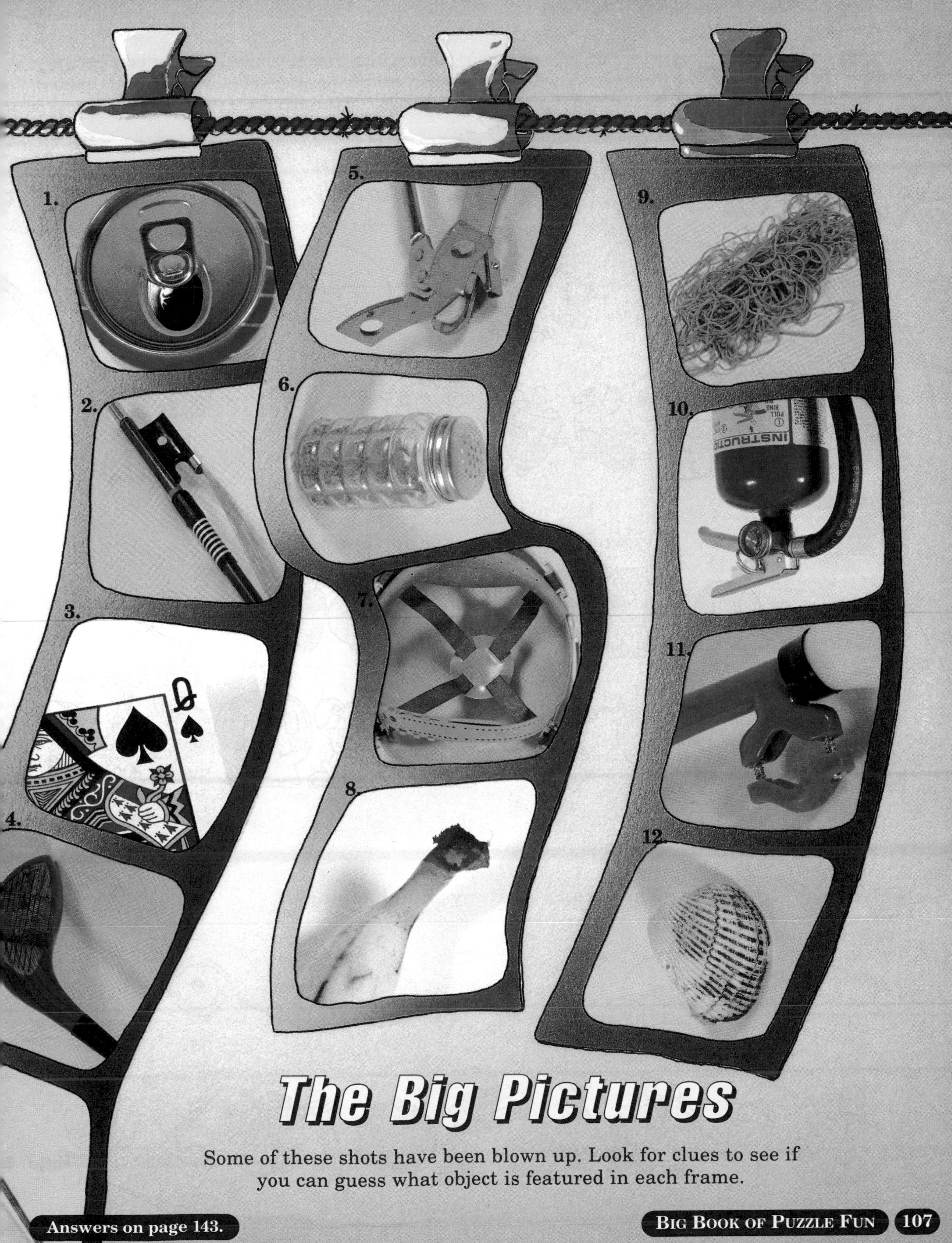

The Big Pictures

Some of these shots have been blown up. Look for clues to see if you can guess what object is featured in each frame.

Answers on page 143.

Crack the Code

For a real crack-up, help Rita decipher the riddle messages below. Each picture stands for the first letter in its word.

What is the center of gravity?

.

Why would you put sugar on your pillow?

.

Where can you always find happiness?

.

Illustrated by Mike Dammer

Float to page 143 for the answer.

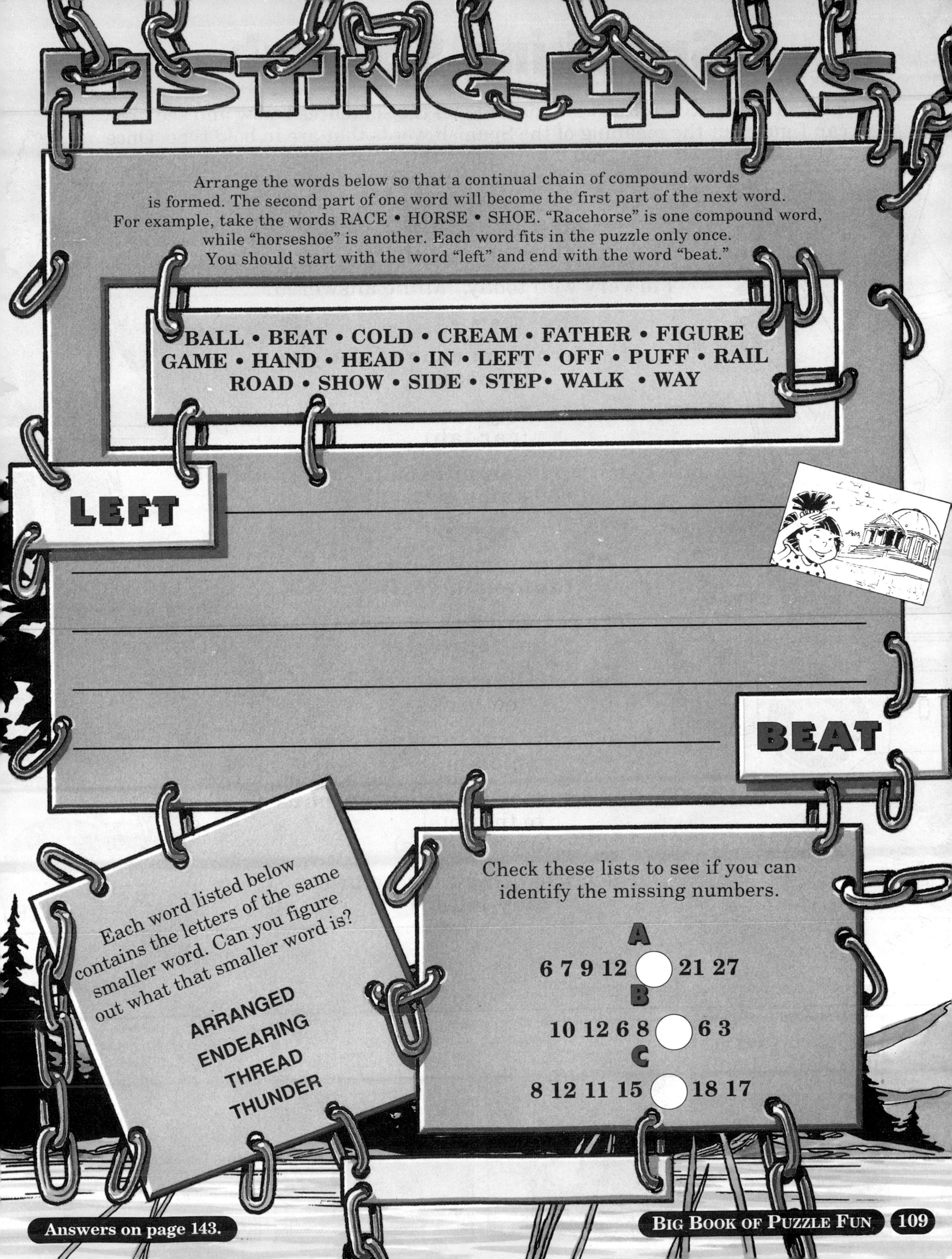

LASTING LINKS

Arrange the words below so that a continual chain of compound words is formed. The second part of one word will become the first part of the next word. For example, take the words RACE • HORSE • SHOE. "Racehorse" is one compound word, while "horseshoe" is another. Each word fits in the puzzle only once. You should start with the word "left" and end with the word "beat."

BALL • BEAT • COLD • CREAM • FATHER • FIGURE GAME • HAND • HEAD • IN • LEFT • OFF • PUFF • RAIL ROAD • SHOW • SIDE • STEP • WALK • WAY

LEFT ______________________________

____

____

____

______________________________ **BEAT**

Each word listed below contains the letters of the same smaller word. Can you figure out what that smaller word is?

ARRANGED
ENDEARING
THREAD
THUNDER

Check these lists to see if you can identify the missing numbers.

A

6 7 9 12 ◯ 21 27

B

10 12 6 8 ◯ 6 3

C

8 12 11 15 ◯ 18 17

Answers on page 143.

Speaking Spanish

Spanish is Mexico's official language. Read the sentences below and see if you can figure out the meaning of the Spanish words that are in bold type. Once you get them all right, you'll have some new words to try on your friends.

"¿**Como estas**?" Lee asked.
(ko-mo ess-tahs)

"I'm very well today," Millie answered.

• • •

"I want a nice red **manzana**," Dotty said.
(monsana)

"Where can I mail my **carta**?" Roy wondered.
(car-tah)

"Be sure to put an **estampilla** on it!" advised Max.
(ess-stamp-pea-ya)

• • •

That **automovil** is fast.
(auto-moh-veal)

The **cotorra** flew overhead.
(ko-tour-ra)

Put your **libros** over there.
(lee-bros)

I can't write without my **pluma**.
(ploo-ma)

The tourists took the yellow **autobus** to the hotel.
(ow-toe-boos)

The pitcher threw the **pelota**.
(pay-loh-ta)

YOU KNOW, IF YOU'VE GOT A PUPPY DOG, HE'LL NEED A LICENSE.

...BUT HE'S NOT A HUNTING DOG!

HAHA! JUST KIDDING! OF COURSE I KNOW WHAT A DOG LICENSE IS!!

A Horse of a Different Color

A horse is a horse, of course, but they don't all look alike. One of the beautiful breeds pictured below doesn't really exist at all! Can you spot the "phony pony"?

A. Appaloosa - This dappled breed was developed by the Nez Perce Indians.
B. Palomino - This graceful golden horse has a pale, flowing mane.
C. Pantella - A breed developed in Spain, known for its striped coat.
D. Percheron - A large French draught horse known for beauty and strength.
E. Pinto - A swift native American breed with clearly divided markings.

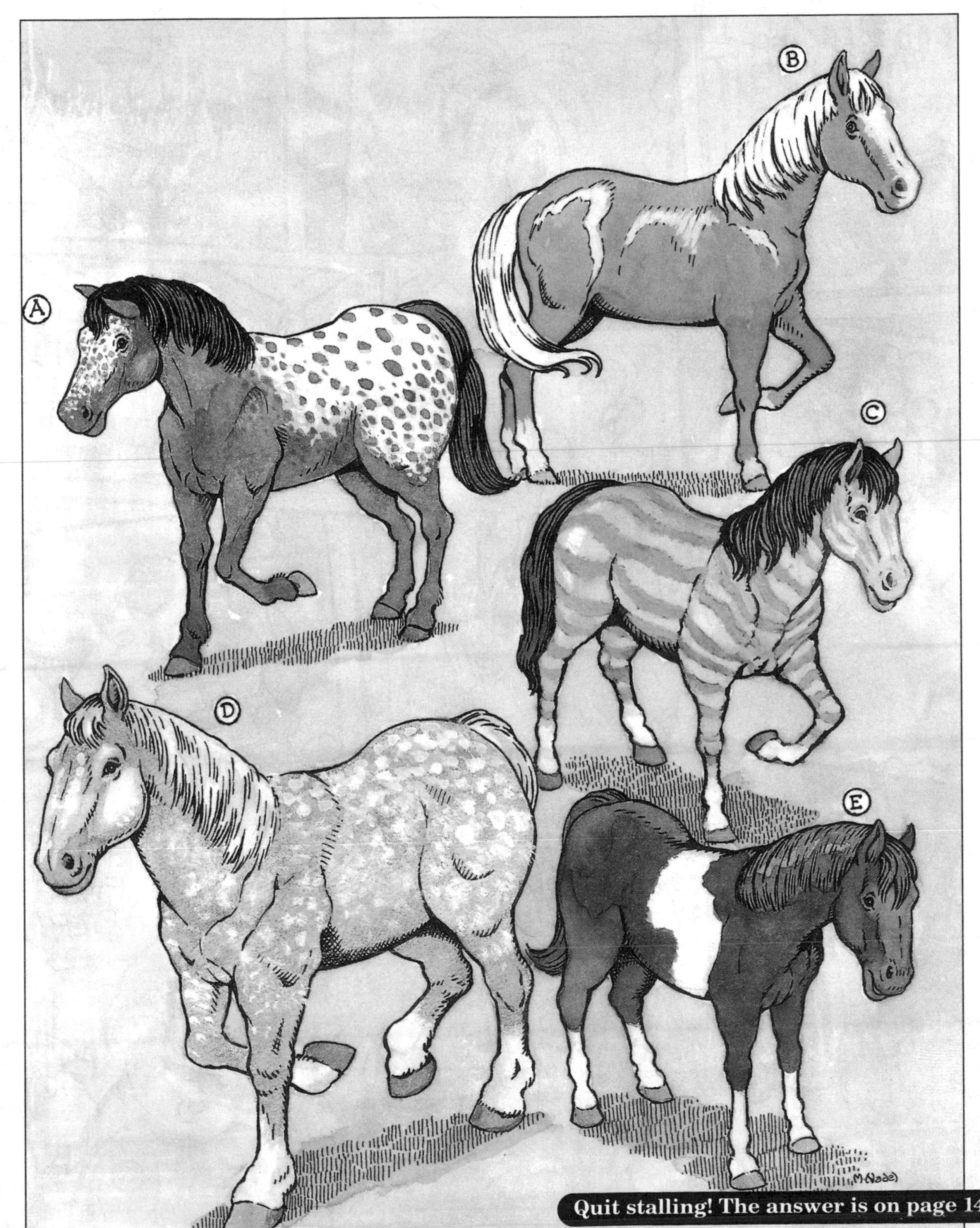

Quit stalling! The answer is on page 143.

TOO MUCH TURKEY!

Too much turkey! How many stomachs will be saying that this Thanksgiving? But never were those words more true than in this puzzle. Turkeys have taken over these famous fairy tales and now the real characters from those stories want their jobs back. See if you can help by matching each character with the correct story.

Illustrated by Jerry Zimmerman

Answers on page 143.

I've Got Plenty of Stuffin'!

All the turkeys that are still around the day after Thanksgiving are having their OWN celebration. And you can surely guess what they're celebrating. But can you guess that THEY are eating? Is it breast of bagel or filet of flapjacks? Draw in their dinner. We'd like to see what you're serving.

DOTTY

Connect these dots to find an inappropriate entertainer at any Thanksgiving feast.

Answer on page 143.

Something I Ate...

Rambyte would always be hungry if all he had to eat were his own words. But he's full now because all of the words in this puzzle contain the letters **A-T-E**.

Use the clues and see how many words you can figure ate, er . . . we mean figure out. Some clues are tricky, so look for double meanings.

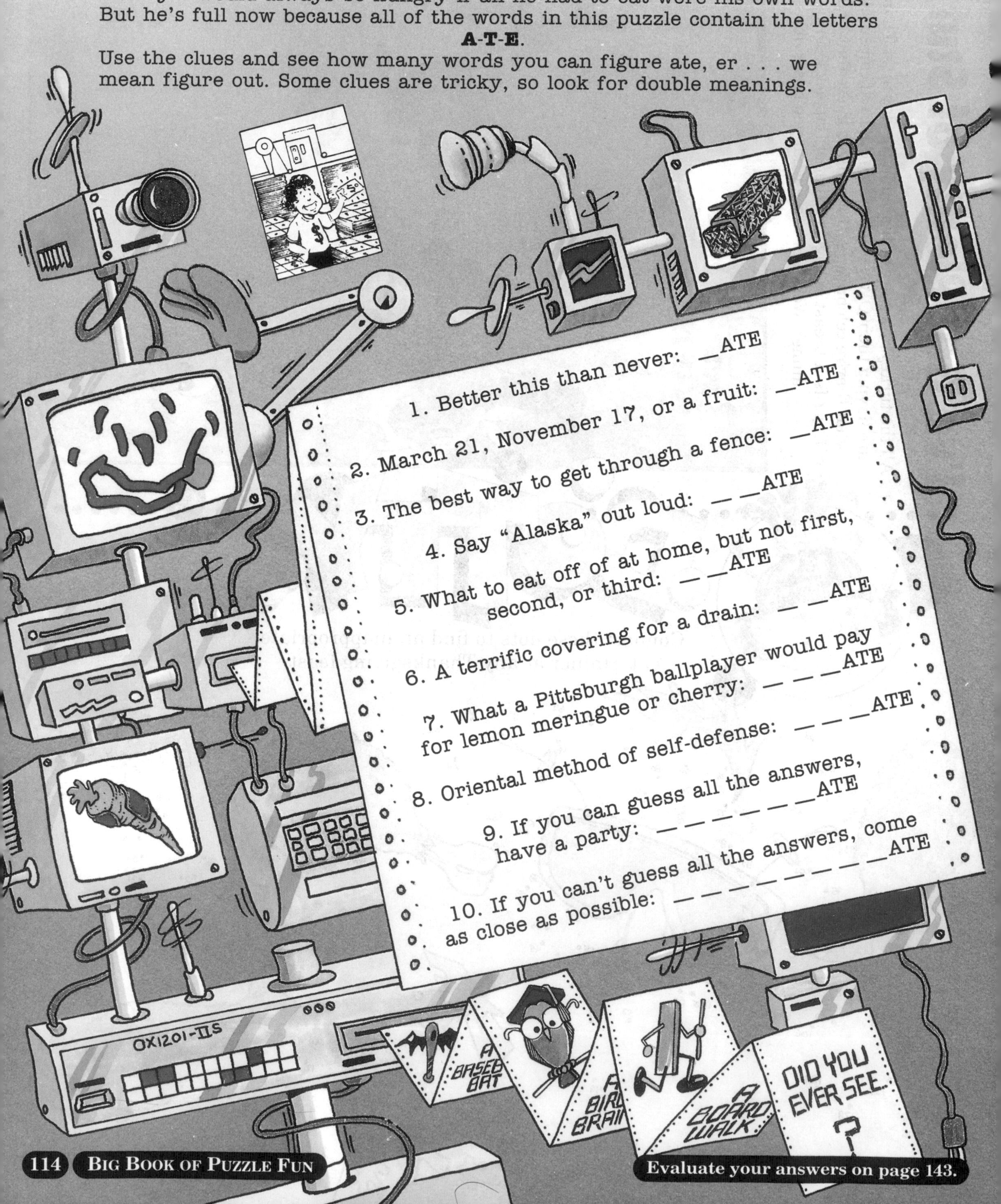

1. Better this than never: _ATE
2. March 21, November 17, or a fruit: _ATE
3. The best way to get through a fence: _ATE
4. Say "Alaska" out loud: _ _ATE
5. What to eat off of at home, but not first, second, or third: _ _ATE
6. A terrific covering for a drain: _ _ATE
7. What a Pittsburgh ballplayer would pay for lemon meringue or cherry: _ _ _ATE
8. Oriental method of self-defense: _ _ _ATE
9. If you can guess all the answers, have a party: _ _ _ _ _ _ATE
10. If you can't guess all the answers, come as close as possible: _ _ _ _ _ _ _ _ _ATE
OX1201-IIS
A BASEBALL BAT
A BIRD BRAIN
A BOARD WALK
DID YOU EVER SEE...
?

Evaluate your answers on page 143.

Nature Hike

One letter of the alphabet can be inserted in each blank below so that a new word will appear. Each word will be something you might see while on a nature hike in the woods. Not all letters in a certain line will be needed to make a new word. Each letter of the alphabet will be used only once, so cross the letter off when you find a place for it. The first one is done to start you on your hike.

A B C D E F G H I J K L M N O P Q R S T U V W X Y Z

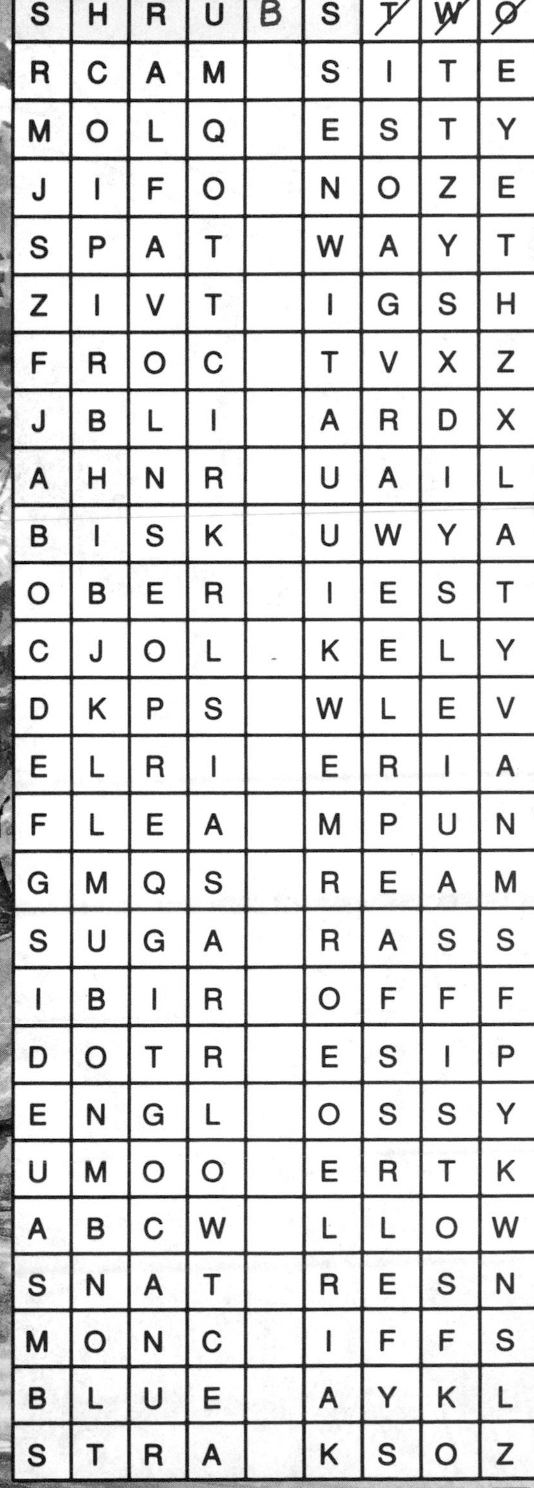

S	H	R	U	B	S	T	W	O
R	C	A	M		S	I	T	E
M	O	L	Q		E	S	T	Y
J	I	F	O		N	O	Z	E
S	P	A	T		W	A	Y	T
Z	I	V	T		I	G	S	H
F	R	O	C		T	V	X	Z
J	B	L	I		A	R	D	X
A	H	N	R		U	A	I	L
B	I	S	K		U	W	Y	A
O	B	E	R		I	E	S	T
C	J	O	L		K	E	L	Y
D	K	P	S		W	L	E	V
E	L	R	I		E	R	I	A
F	L	E	A		M	P	U	N
G	M	Q	S		R	E	A	M
S	U	G	A		R	A	S	S
I	B	I	R		O	F	F	F
D	O	T	R		E	S	I	P
E	N	G	L		O	S	S	Y
U	M	O	O		E	R	T	K
A	B	C	W		L	L	O	W
S	N	A	T		R	E	S	N
M	O	N	C		I	F	F	S
B	L	U	E		A	Y	K	L
S	T	R	A		K	S	O	Z

Hike over to page 143 for the answer.

Pumpkin Picking

How many pumpkins can you pick
from this page?

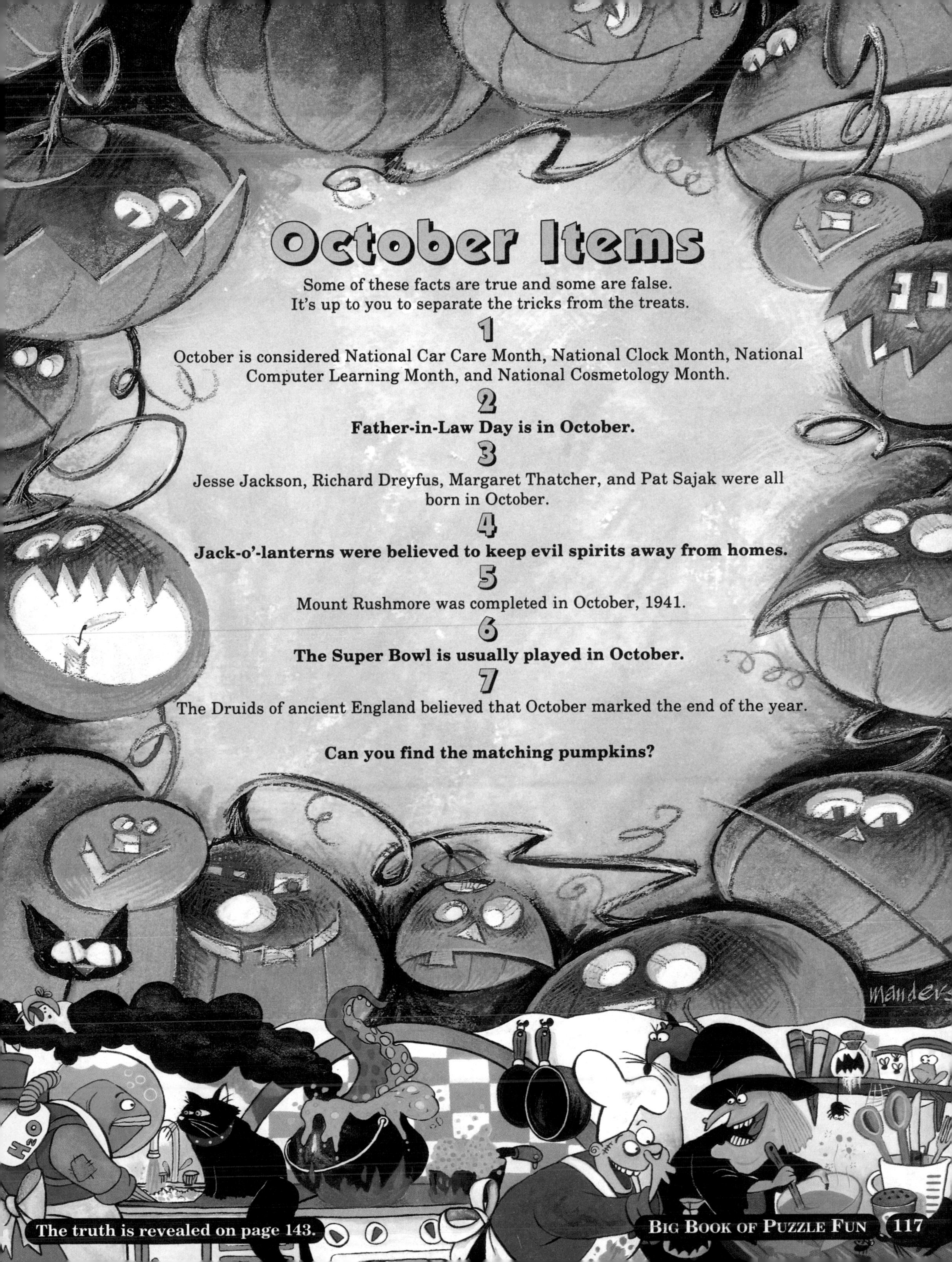

October Items

Some of these facts are true and some are false.
It's up to you to separate the tricks from the treats.

1

October is considered National Car Care Month, National Clock Month, National Computer Learning Month, and National Cosmetology Month.

2

Father-in-Law Day is in October.

3

Jesse Jackson, Richard Dreyfus, Margaret Thatcher, and Pat Sajak were all born in October.

4

Jack-o'-lanterns were believed to keep evil spirits away from homes.

5

Mount Rushmore was completed in October, 1941.

6

The Super Bowl is usually played in October.

7

The Druids of ancient England believed that October marked the end of the year.

Can you find the matching pumpkins?

The truth is revealed on page 143.

FALL FOUL-UP

Ah, 'tis autumn, bringing with it brightly colored leaves, pumpkin pies, apple cider, surfing at the beach . . . surfing at the beach? What's going on here? See if you can find what's out of season in this fall picture.

THE Huddle Befuddle

The Puzzle Pals were in the middle of the biggest football game of the fall. "Now here's the play," barked Lee in the huddle. "This one can't miss. Millie, go out to Max's bike and cut into the middle. Rita, go straight up the middle and cut over to Roy's sweatshirt. Brian, go into the end zone and head for the goal post. Holly, go out to Linc's hat and turn around. Roy, you stay in and block. Ready—on two—break!"

Which picture shows Lee's play?

Answer on page 143.

Mystery Want Ads

Each of these mystery want ads should remind you of a rhyme, song, or story. How many can you recognize?

Lost and Found

1. LOST—Runaway dish and spoon, needed by music-loving cat.
2. LOST—Sheep. Owner is very sad.
3. FOUND—One pair of shoes and small jacket, near Mr. McGregor's garden.
4. FOUND—Glass slipper, on palace steps.

Help Wanted

5. GUIDE—Needed by girl for journey through forest where wolf lives. Wants to take basket of food to grandmother.
6. WORKERS—To repair large bridge. Apply at Buckingham Palace.

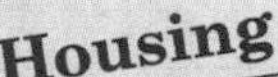

Housing

7. WANTED TO BUY—Sturdy, well-built house for three brothers. Must be able to stand up to strong winds.
8. FOR SALE—Strangely shaped house, too small for woman with very large family.

Legal Notices

9. REWARD—For information leading to capture of the knave who stole tarts from the royal kitchen.
10. WANTED—Need information from anyone who saw a boy running through town in his nightgown.

Answers on page 144.

What Does That Mean?

Can you tell what phrase or word is shown in each picture?

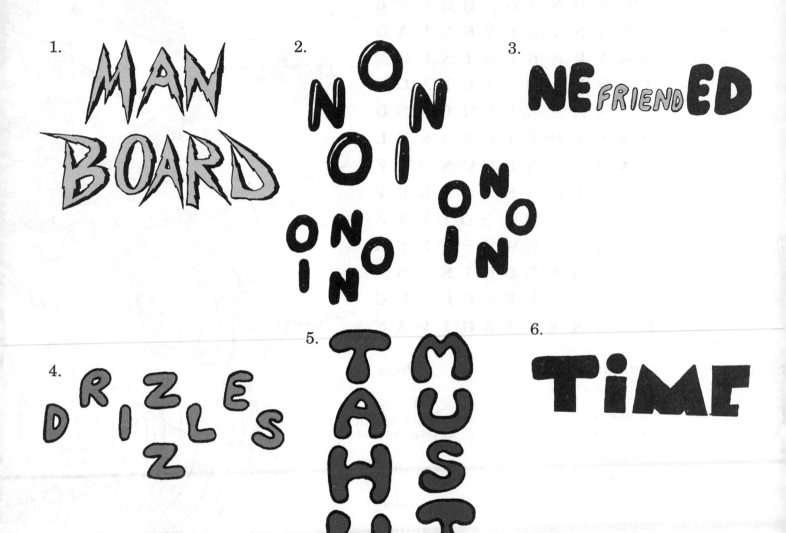

1. 2. 3.

4.

DRIZZLES

5.

T A H W

M U S T

6.

TiME

7.

THE WEATHER
FEELING

8.

miBnuUte

9.

The translations are on page 144.

New World Search

While Columbus searches for new worlds, you should search this puzzle for new words that tell all about this famous explorer. Look up, down, across, backward, and diagonally to find facts about Columbus. Then read the leftover letters to learn the name of one of Columbus's friends and patrons.

I M F D N A N I D R E F B

A S A N T A P Y E L L A G

N A A R N S P A I N R R M

I I N B I O U I L T A D O

N L R A E A L S H O A N O

O S N T M L I O A R S U L

C A D N T A L N C N O O E

I C L I N O E A D I N R V

N I R P M N G S O I E A A

E A O E D E W E S T E E R

M M W M A G G N I K U S A

O A P I L E F R C D Q H C

D J E N A E T A G I V A N

Birthplace
Genoa

Father
Domenico

Mother
Susanna

Brothers
Bartholomew
Diego

Wife
Felipa

Sponsors
King Ferdinand
(2 separate words)
Queen Isabella
(2 separate words)
Spain

Worked for Father
Loom

His Spanish Name
Colon

Ships
Niña
Pinta
Santa Maria
(2 separate words)
caravel
galley
oars
sails

Abilities
navigate
seaman

Places Scouted
Around world
(2 separate words)
Indies
Jamaica
west

Left Port on First Voyage
Palos (Spain)

His Patron

____

Sail to page 144 for the answers.

The Ocean Commotion

To celebrate the 500th anniversary of Columbus's explorations of the New World, we are re-creating his famous voyage. Everything's in place—the Niña, the Pinta, even the Santa Maria. The only thing missing is Linc. Hurry and find him so Chris can set sail. Also discover a cat, a candle, and a cook.

Snow Row Row

The Puzzle Pals spent all morning playing in the snow. You may notice that each row of snow people has something in common. For example, in the top row across, each snowman has a carrot nose. Look at the other rows, across, down, or diagonally. Do you snow what each row has in common?

The answer is frozen on page 144.

 Snow Code 

Using this snowflake alphabet, see if you can figure out what these skaters are saying.

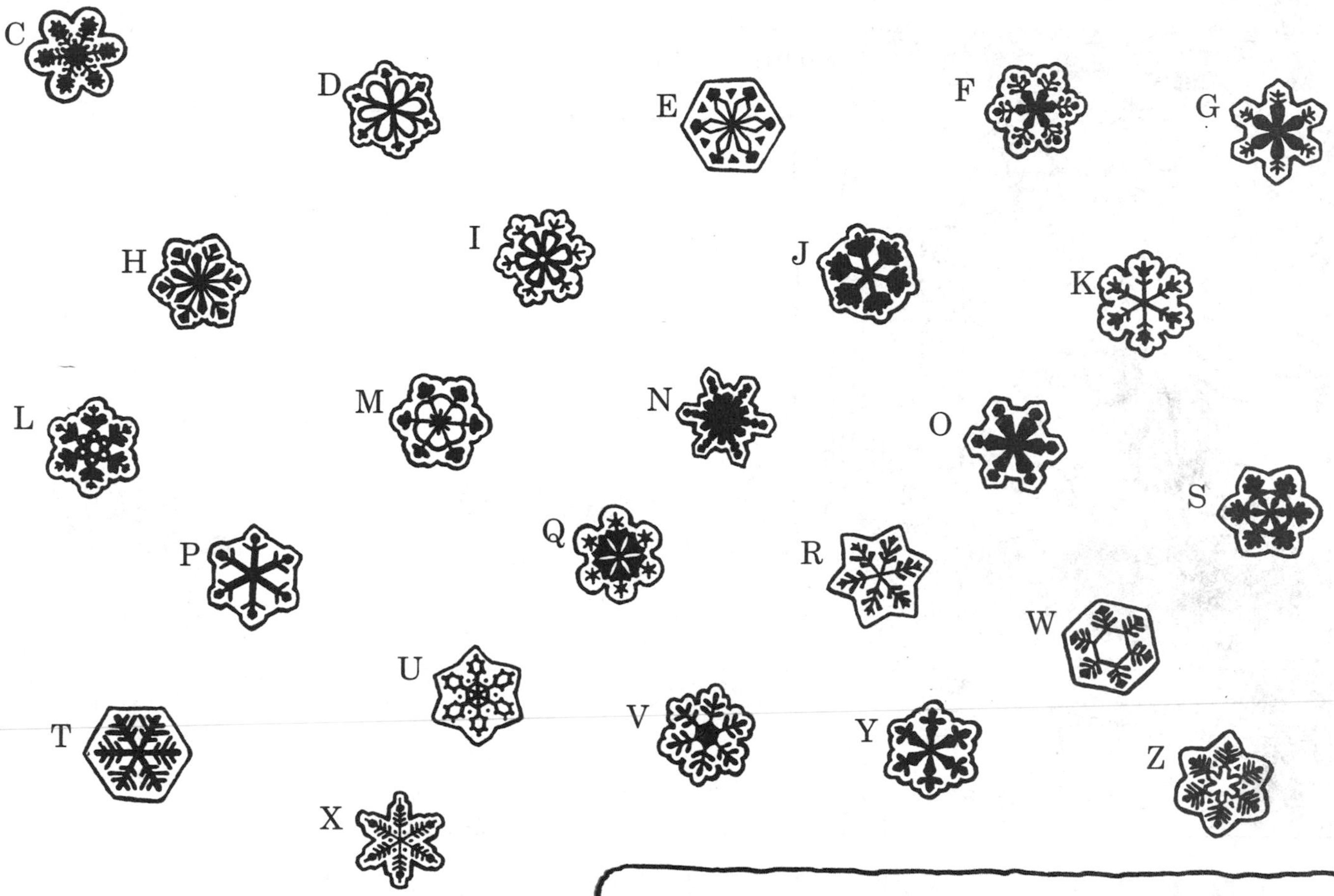

C D E F G H I J K L M N O S P Q R W U T V Y Z X

SALE PRICES INCLUDE TAX

Money Matters I

Logical Lee is shopping at the Smart Money Mart to buy gifts for his dad, Cousin Dan, and Aunt Rae. He has exactly $30.03 to spend. Using the list of clues he's holding, help Lee decide what gift each person might like that is also within his budget.

	Dad	Cousin Dan	Aunt Rae
likes	cars	games	bugs
dislikes	green	batteries	glue

Money Matters II

Even though she had to spend a little of it, Dotty managed to save most of her money to buy presents. Look through her list and let her know how much she has to spend.

Baby-sitting job	+12.00
Walked neighbor's dog	+ 2.50
Bought new dotted shirt	- 6.75
Got a check from Grandma	+10.00
Purchased "Thank You" card and stamp	- 1.35 - .29
Allowance	+ 5.00
Joined school book club	- 2.25
Total $	

These all add up on page 144.

Holiday Shopping

The Cratchits are having a party this Christmas. Big Bill Cratchit, the oldest son, is out doing the shopping, but he's having some trouble. He has to pick up each item on his list in the exact order given. Also, Mrs. Cratchit wants him to hurry, so Bill isn't allowed to cross over or retrace his own path. Can you help him find the correct path that will lead him to all eight stores in the proper order?

Present for Tiny Tim.
Pick up Dad's new suit.
Get candy for the table.
We need decorations for the house.
Buy Dad a new hammer.
Don't forget the turkey!
Choose a hot pumpkin pie.
Bring Mom fresh flowers.

Illustrated by Bill Basso

Tree Trimmings

Which light on this tree is ready to be plugged in?

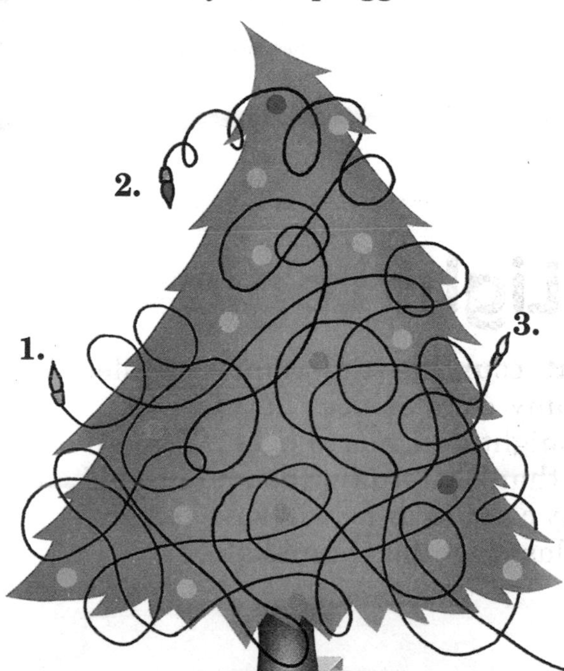

Light up the answers on page 144.

Dot Connection

This family is getting ready to celebrate the first night of Hanukkah. Can you connect the dots to find some traditional items for this holiday?

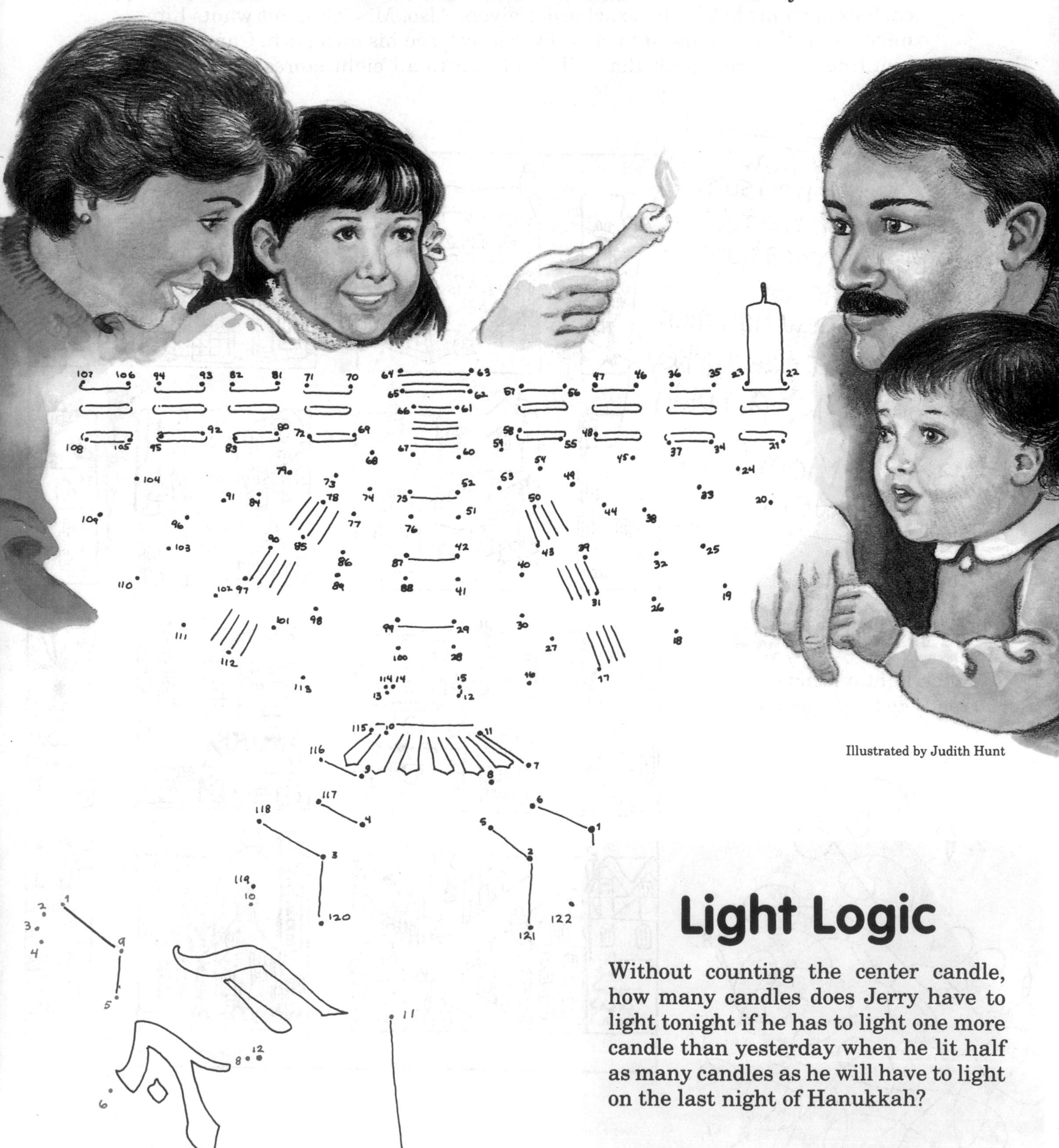

Illustrated by Judith Hunt

Light Logic

Without counting the center candle, how many candles does Jerry have to light tonight if he has to light one more candle than yesterday when he lit half as many candles as he will have to light on the last night of Hanukkah?

Answers on page 144.

SOME THINGS NEVER CHANGE

These pictures may all look different, but there are four objects that are in all four scenes. Can you figure out what they are?

Illustrated by Allan Eitzen

Answers on page 144.

TOBOGGAN TROUBLE

There are at least 25 objects hidden in this large picture. How many can you find?

Holiday Wrap Up

All of these letters were hung with care in the hope that the Puzzle Pals soon would be here. Words of the holidays are all in this grid. Search up, down, across, diagonally, and backward to find where they're hid.

- Celebration
- Candles
- Christmas
- Dance
- Dreidel
- First Crops
- Gifts
- Hanukkah
- Harvest
- Joy
- Karamu
- Kinara
- Kislev
- Kwanzaa
- Menorah
- Mistletoe
- Shammash
- Stocking
- Tinsel
- Tree

U	M	I	S	T	L	E	T	O	E	D	A
N	M	H	A	N	U	K	K	A	H	J	S
S	H	A	M	M	A	S	H	X	A	S	P
V	H	R	R	N	Q	Y	D	S	A	T	O
O	A	V	V	A	O	T	A	W	Z	O	R
S	R	E	E	J	K	M	N	S	N	C	C
E	O	S	L	R	T	L	C	E	A	K	T
L	N	T	S	S	L	C	E	D	W	I	S
D	E	K	I	N	A	R	A	S	K	N	R
N	M	R	K	S	T	F	I	G	N	G	I
A	H	D	R	E	I	D	E	L	R	I	F
C	E	L	E	B	R	A	T	I	O	N	T

Art: Jeff Shelly

The answer is presented on page 144.

Shovel Trouble

Help these shovelers get home by following their paths back to the right houses. Some paths may cross, but no shoveler's direction changes at a right angle.

Dig over to page 144 for the answer.

REPEAT THAT, PLEASE!

Can you find seven things that look the same in both of these pictures?

Illustrated by Allan Eitzen

Farm Fun

To find out what cows say to each other at midnight on December 31, follow the instructions below.

1. How many reindeer does Santa have, including Rudolph?
   If less than 7, put an A in the spaces marked VII and X.
   If more than 7, put an A in spaces II and XI.

2. Kwanzaa is a holiday celebrated by African-Americans.
   If it's celebrated in the winter, put an M in space VI.
   If it's celebrated in the spring, put an M in space III.

3. What brought Frosty the Snowman to life?
   If it was a red scarf, put an R in space V.
   If it was an old silk hat, put an R in space XII.

4. People are supposed to get a kiss under a certain plant during this holiday season.
   If the plant is mistletoe, put an H in space I.
   If the plant is poinsettia, put an H in space VIII.

5. When "the weather outside is frightful," what should we do?
   If we should "let it snow," put an E in space X.
   If we should "grab a shovel," put an E in space IV.

6. Hanukkah can be known by another name.
   If it is the "Festival of Winter," put a P in spaces IX and V.
   If it is the "Festival of Lights," put a P in spaces III and IV.

7. Joyeux Noel means Merry Christmas in what language?
   If French, put a Y in spaces V and IX.
   If Spanish, put a Y in spaces VIII and XII.

8. What was Scrooge's first name?
   If Fred, put an O in spaces I and II.
   If Ebenezer, put an O in spaces VII and VIII.

What do the cows say?

___ ___ ___ ___ ___   ___ ___ ___   ___ ___ ___ ___
I II III IV V   VI VII VIII   IX X XI XII

Illustrated by R. Michael Palan

The answer will greet you on page 144.

Echo Match

Every item below can be matched with one other item that has the same sound. Can you find all six pairs?

Every item below can be matched with one other item that has the same sound. Can you find all six pairs?

Echo Match

Answers on page 144.

Christmas Crossword

This puzzle features questions about many of the songs and stories of the Christmas holiday.

1 2 3 4 5
6 7 8
9 10
11
12 13 14 15
16
17 18 19
20 21 22
23 24
25 26 27
28
29

ACROSS

1. "It came upon a _______ clear"
7. "____ beginning to look a lot like Christmas"
9. Percussion instrument played by little boy
10. Number of times Santa will check his list
12. Miser from "A Christmas Carol"
13. Santa's entrance to a house
16. "I tossed back the shutter and threw up the ____"
18. "They used to laugh and call him _____"
20. Kisses are exchanged beneath this plant
21. Three of them were from the Orient
23. Material of which the little soldier was made
25. Hot drink for winter
27. Reindeer who became famous one foggy eve
28. Santa's helpers
29. People put presents under this

DOWN

1. Not even this creature was stirring
2. Christmas ballet
3. He stole Christmas
4. Put a ribbon in place
5. Foxy reindeer
6. German name for Santa Claus
8. Snowflake dressed in a gown
9. Hang a wreath here
11. Famous dancing snowman
14. Places for travelers to stay
15. The night before Christmas
17. Santa's workshop is at the North ____
19. Father's partner
22. You could even say Rudolph's nose does this
24. Number of reindeer on Santa's team
25. Tiny character of Dickens book
26. Song title: "___ Maria"

Answers on page 144.

Cover

The fish here are butterfly fish, catfish, dogfish, oarfish (or paddlefish), parrotfish, sailfish, sawfish, starfish, sunfish, swordfish.

At The Big Top (pages 2-3)

Giraffe Maze (page 5)

Nose and Toes Match-Up (page 6)

1. D-camel
2. C-warthog
3. E-ostrich
4. A-water buffalo
5. G-flamingo
6. F-zebra
7. H-giraffe
8. B-elephant

Animal Catchphrases (page 7)

1. tHEN
2. bOWL
3. PIGeon
4. gRATe
5. CATcher
6. OXygen
7. giANT
8. grAPE
9. COWardly
10. milLION

Jungle Jumble (page 8)

horse, seal, leopard
dog, giraffe, ferret
tiger, gerbil
cow, wolf, fox
narwhal, whale, emu, mule
elephant, ant, antelope
gorilla, llama
okapi, pig, iguana

Shadowy Shapes (page 9)

Zoo Clues (pages 10-11)

Where do spies sleep? UNDERCOVERS

What's to Eat? (page 13)

X O F D E R E H S I F N
O W O L V E R I N E O I
F B M E N I M R E I T T
Y A L G R I Z Z L Y T R
A D I E E A T N R A E A
R G T T S O I A C S R M
G E A B L A C K B E A R
L R O E T C E O E A A K
Y T C N O G E W Y L R N
N O U O O T A C B O B I
X O N D T E R R E F T M
M F L O W R E B M I T E

A carnivore is a MEAT EATER.

When I Grow Up (page 13)

1. Deer 2. Cow 3. Horse 4. Swan
5. Goose 6. Sheep 7. Goat 8. Frog
9. Duck 10. Kangaroo

Meg's Magical Mystery Paint (page 14)

KANGAROO
GIRAFFE
ZEBRA
PENGUIN
ELEPHANT
LEOPARD
TURTLE
GORILLA
EAGLE
CHEETAH

Sing a Little Tuna (page 16)

"Take Meow to the Ball Game"

Wanna Bet? (page 16)

Each egg still takes 10 minutes to become hard-boiled.

Doubled Dragons (page 17)

2 and 5 match.

Ant Antics (page 17)

Riddle Rhymes (page 19)

1. You can't shut the door.
2. I don't know, but if it stings you, you're in real trouble.
3. So it can hide in a strawberry patch.
4. They always have their trunks with them.
5. Orange juice
6. Time to get a new bed

Port of Call (page 20)

Continental Drift (page 21)

1. supPER Until - Peru
2. speeCH IN Atlanta - China
3. CurtiS PAINted - Spain
4. nICE LANDing - Iceland
5. taKEN YAms - Kenya
6. WeB, OLIVIA? - Bolivia
7. IN DIAna's - India
8. J.J. OR DANny - Jordan
9. CAN ADA - Canada
10. MAL Is? - Mali
11. TO GO - Togo
12. aGREE, CEcily? - Greece

Mountain Match (page 22)

Fuji - Japan
Everest - Nepal
Rushmore - South Dakota
Kilimanjaro - Tanzania
McKinley - Alaska
Mont Blanc - France
Matterhorn - Switzerland
Shasta - California
Pike's Peak - Colorado
Etna - Italy

Word Wise (page 24)

1. Incorrectally should be incorrectly.
2. All 12 months have 28 days. Most have more.
3. 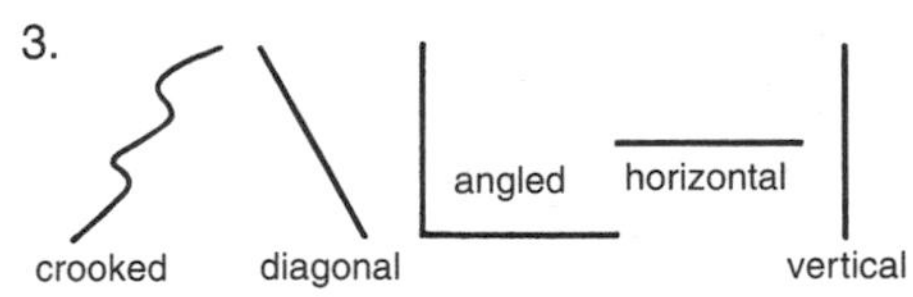

4. H, I, and M can all be drawn using only straight lines.
5. H, I, S, and O all look the same either upside down or rightside up.
6. P

Magna-Search (page 25)

Money Matters (page 26)

1. $10.00
2. Car
3. $4.20

Tape Time (page 26)

Lee needs a 75-minute tape.

Clipped Coupons (page 27)

1-A 2-F 3-B 4-G 5-D 6-C 7-E

Wrong Ring-Up (page 27)

C

Side Stack (page 27)

C

You're Invited (page 28)

1. Pluto 2. Mercury 3. Mars
4. Jupiter 5. Saturn 6. Venus
7. Neptune 8. Uranus 9. Earth

Unearthly Hares (page 28)

1. Hair dryer 2. Hair brush
3. Snowshoe hare

Planet Pals (page 29)

1-D 2-B 3-F 4-C 5-E 6-A

At Friday's Footwear (page 30)

1- New Year's Day - January
2- Groundhog Day - February
4- Independence Day - July
5- Labor Day - September
6- Election Day - November
7- Hanukkah - December
8- Rosh Hashanah - September
9- Good Friday - April
11- Mother's Day - May
12- Columbus Day - October
14- Valentine's Day - February
15- MLK's Birthday - January
17- St. Patrick's Day - March
18- Father's Day - June
19- President's Day - February
20- First day of Spring - March
21- Ash Wednesday - March
22- Thanksgiving - November
25- Christmas - December
26- Memorial Day - May
29- Passover - April
31 - Halloween - October

Fun Days (page 31)

1-real	16-arcade	31-canal
2-cane	17-clear	
3-darn	18-dance	
4-land	19-learn	
5-clean	20-dear	
6-race	21-den	
7-cradle	22-candle	
8-near	23-read	
9-lead	24-crane	
10-lane	25-lend	
11-ace	26-care	
12-dare	27-lard	
13-lad	28-decal	
14-deal	29-lance	
15-card	30-end	

Spring Things (page 32)

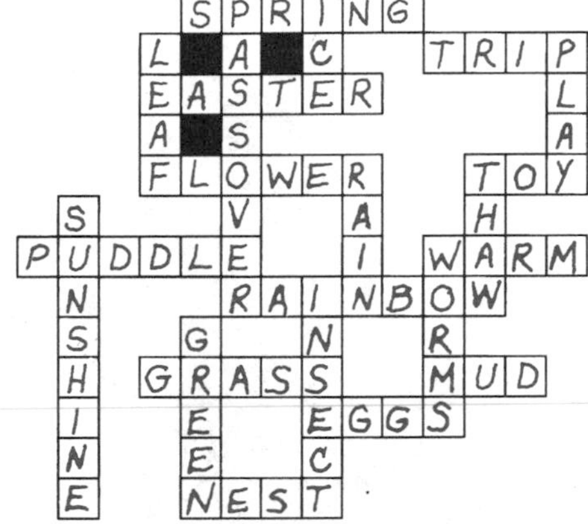

Colorful Names (page 34)

A-sepia	G-periwinkle
B-lavender	H-magenta
C-ochre	I-crimson
D-emerald	J-beige
E-cyan	K-vermillion
F-chartreuse	L-teal

Whose Flower Is That? (page 34)

1. magnolia 5. begonia
2. poinsettia 6. forsythia
3. zinnia 7. dahlia
4. camellia 8. gardenia

Rhyme Time (page 35)

2. Heel, peel
3. Tape, nape
4. Neat, heat
5. SH

Fortune Hunting (page 36)

The Leopard... Does not change his spots.

If you can't ride two horses... You shouldn't be in the circus.

You stay with the girl... You brought to the dance.

A journey of 1,000 miles... Begins with just a single step.

A moneyless man... Goes fast through the market.

You cannot put an old head... On young shoulders.

The shoemaker's son... Always goes barefoot.

A golden key... Can open any door.

A cat who wears gloves... Catches no mice.

Cog Clog (page 37)

Riddle Me These (page 38)

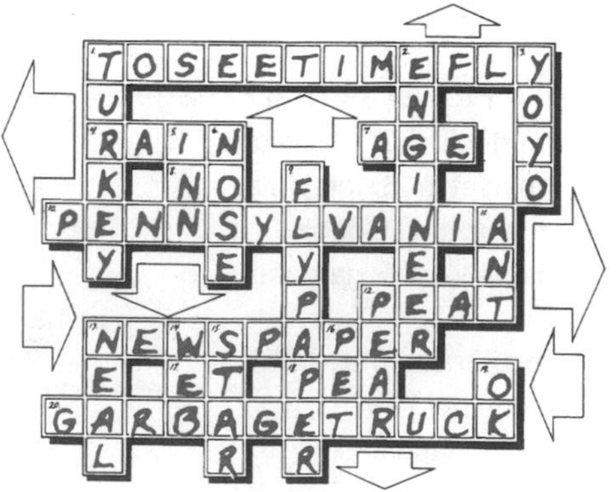

Buying a Bonnet (page 39)

Brain Teasers (page 40)

1. Sheep
2. Neither. 8+7=15
3. S. The first initials of the days of the week.
4. Verbs - run, build, think. Nouns - cat, man, frog. Under some circumstances, man may also be a verb.
5. If the races haven't happened yet, Matt can't watch them on TV tonight.
6. Eddie lost a mitten, but Grandma's knitting a hat.
7. The car sped off when the light turned red.

Mum's the Word (page 41)

1. Carnation
2. Tulips
3. Marigold
4. Gladiolas
5. Violet
6. Lilacs
7. Rhododendron

Setting Up Camp (page 41)

C-A-E-D-F-B

Food Find (page 42)

1. Jelly
2. Beans
3. Gravy
4. Stuffing
5. Cookies
6. Eggs
7. Cabbage
8. Danish
9. Meatballs
10. French fries
11. Crackers
12. Tomato
13. Butter
14. Strawberry
15. Cream cheese
16. Cheese
17. Cake
18. Syrup

C	R	E	A	M	C	H	E	E	S	E
S	E	I	R	F	H	C	N	E	R	F
L	C	T	O	T	A	M	O	T	J	Z
L	R	H	E	G	A	B	B	A	C	G
A	A	S	C	O	O	K	I	E	S	N
B	C	I	A	E	G	M	F	G	O	I
T	K	N	K	S	J	R	T	G	I	F
A	E	A	E	E	B	E	A	S	T	F
E	R	D	L	E	S	T	L	V	O	U
M	S	L	A	H	W	T	U	L	Y	T
V	Y	N	Z	C	P	U	R	Y	S	S
K	S	T	R	A	W	B	E	R	R	Y

Fun Puns (page 44)

1. Leftovers
2. Orange juice
3. Narrow escape
4. Middle of the night
5. Running on empty
6. Top hat

Breakfast Baffler (page 44)

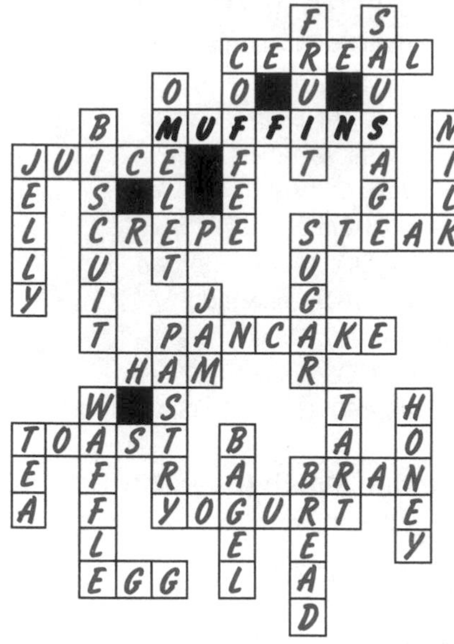

Don't Be Negative (page 45)

A-H B-G C-E D-F

Pancake Puzzle (page 45)

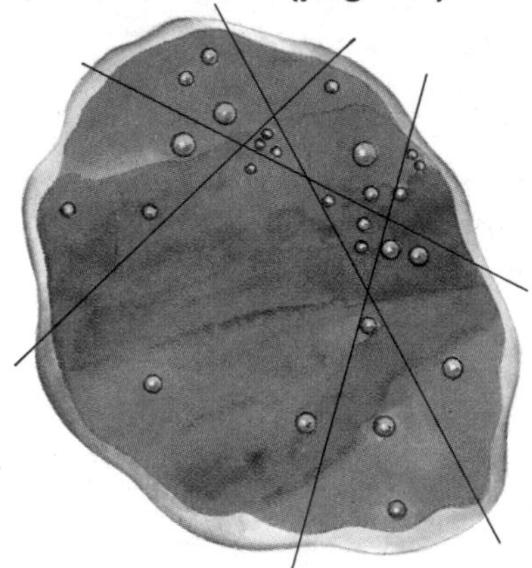

Perplexing Puzzles (page 46)

Here are some choices we found. You may have found others.

1. Pear, peach
2. Panda, pig
3. Petunia, phlox
4. Pea, pumpkin
5. Police officer, postal worker
6. Puzzle, puppet
7. Pajamas, pullovers
8. Pens, pencils

Tongue Twister

Peter Piper picked a peck of pickled peppers. A peck of pickled peppers Peter Piper picked.

Fill in the Blanks.

1. Apple
2. Pepperoni
3. Flippers
4. Sloppy
5. Puppy
6. Mississippi
7. Opposites
8. Happy
9. Applaud
10. Hippopotamus

Coin Exchange (page 48)

Lelani should give one penny to Travis and Juan should give one dime to Lelani.

Write the Headline (page 48)

1. T	4. T	7. F	10. F
2. F	5. T	8. T	11. T
3. F	6. F	9. F	12. T

Headline: FIRST WOMAN ACROSS ATLANTIC

Weather Words (page 49)

1. It's April showers that bring May flowers.
2. If you look in one of the columns down, you will find WATER.
3. Sunny, fair, sleet, cold, rain, hail, warm, snow
4. A- cent, tick, grade = centigrade
   B- fare, in, height = fahrenheit

The Blubber-Buster (page 51)

Moose
wAlrus
pygmY owl
cariBou
porcupinE
horneD puffin
mountaIn goat
Coyote
musK ox

Who's the most indecisive whale in the world? MAYBE DICK

Hugaliceos (page 53)

grandmother	Whistler's Mother
mother-of-pearl	Mother Hubbard
mother-in-law	foster mother
Mother Goose	stepmother
Mother Teresa	motherhood

Bread - Because bread is a necessity, and necessity is the "mother" of invention.

The Agony of the Feet (page 54)

That's Shoe Business (page 55)

```
           W
       BROGAN   R
           D    O
         CLEAT FLATS
PUMP   H   R O  L  A
  O  SKIS  SNEAKER N
  C    G     S  R  D
L C    HORSESHOES  A
O A    T     O  K  L
A S   BOOT ICESKATES
FLIPFLOP     S  T
E N   O       C E
R     T     GALOSHES
S   SLIPPERS  O
      E     HIGHHEELS
```

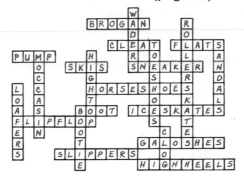

Go for the Gold (page 56)

```
F I R S T L U A V E L O P
S H O T P U T R A C K M X
O C W O R H T R E M M A H
C A I P W S Y R E H C R A
C N N T U R P L U G E A N
E O G C S D I V I N G T D
R E S N J A V E L I N H B
I I K S I N N E T X E O A
D N Y A L E R M O O T N L
I G B V O L L E Y B A L L
N O L O P M U J H G I H Z
G N I T H C A Y E K C O H
```

Going for the Hold (page 57)

Headgear (page 58)

A. Indianapolis Colts	F. Cincinnati Bengals
B. Houston Spurs	G. Toronto Maple Leafs
C. Boston Celtics	H. Chicago Blackhawks
D. Minnesota Vikings	I. Pittsburgh Penguins
E. Chicago Bulls	J. San Jose Sharks

What a Dive! (page 58)

Gold - Clem	Silver - Jane
Bronze - Flo	Forget it! - Willie

Hoop-Hoop-Hooray (page 60)

Barkley Bears - 78 Tiffany Tigers - 81

Build-a-Bike Maze (page 61)

Casey at the Bat (page 62)

In order, the words are:

nine	doffed
play	teeth
game	bat
yell	ball
plate	sun
place	band
smile	out

Let's Play (page 64)

mallet - croquet	table - billiards
racket - tennis	backboard - basketball
helmet - football	stick - hockey
club - golf	paddle - table tennis
ball - soccer	bat - baseball

Home Run Derby (page 64)

Wayne played in 7 games and had 4 home runs.
Pepe played in 9 games and had 3 home runs
Hans played in 8 games and had 4 home runs.
Jennifer played in 4 games and had 8 home runs.

Pepe played in the most games. Jennifer had the most home runs.

Song of the Sea (page 65)

"I've Been Working on the 'Whale' Road"

Seeing Stars (page 65)

We found 42 triangles. How many did you find?

Harvest Signs (page 66)

1. Peas 2. Rice 3. Grapes 4. Melon
5. Blueberries 6. Squash
7. Strawberries 8. String beans

Bubble Trouble (page 66)

1. Bagel
2. Wreath
3. Life preserver
4. Halo
5. Doughnut
6. Hula hoop
7. Ring
8. Inner tube
9. Record
10. Clock

Grandpa's Tall Tales (page 67)

1. A catfish doesn't have a top fin.
2. Copper doesn't rust.

Flight of the Honeybees (page 68)

Checkers Champ (page 69)

1-B 2-E 3-D

Reel Confusion (page 70)

A-3 B-1 C-4 D-2

Film Fun (page 72)

The Invisible Man and
Gone With the Wind

Creature Feature (page 73)

What kind of tryout do they give for horror movies?
A SCREAM TEST

Pop the Question (page 74)

1. Popcorn
2. Pope
3. Poplar
4. Poplin
5. Poppy
6. Population
7. Popular
8. Popeye
9. Lollipop
10. Poppers

What kind of bikes do fathers ride?
POPCYCLES

Going Fourth (page 76)

1. Rhode Island
2. Georgia
3. Pennsylvania
4. New Hampshire
5. New York
6. Virginia
7. New Jersey
8. Connecticut
9. North Carolina
10. Delaware
11. Massachusetts
12. Maryland
13. South Carolina

HAPPY BIRTHDAY, AMERICA!

Crosspatch (page 77)

Which house weighs the least?
A lighthouse.

Mistake at the Museum (page 77)

The five things we found were: the telephone, the radio, the electric light, the toy train, and the fire hydrant. You may have found other items.

Lincoln Logic (page 77)

The flag with the circular stars is the one.

Jumpin' Geography (page 78)

1. Pinch, WV
2. Roll, AZ
3. Chase, MD
4. Load, KY
5. Tow, TX
6. Snowball, AR

Capital Crossword (page 79)

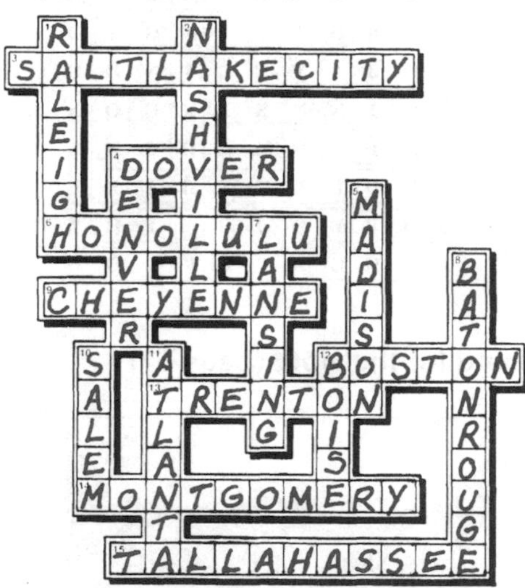

Time Find (page 81)

9	1	2	4	5	2
8	0	5	2	8	5
0	0	0	8	1	9
8	1	6	4	7	8
0	9	3	5	7	6
5	3	6	5	0	3
5	0	2	6	8	5
2	4	5	1	0	2
1	3	1	0	5	5
0	4	0	1	8	1

Word Works (page 82)

1. Eat, ate
2. C and Y
3. Bookkeeper is one, Tallahassee is another
4. Here, hear
5. Wail, whale
6. Write, right, rite

Starry Night (page 84)

There are 10 dark stars, but 11 white stars.

Which Way to Adventure? (page 86)

1 - A - *Alice's Adventures in Wonderland*
2 - D - *Thumbelina*
3 - B - *Robin Hood*
4 - E - *Peter Pan*
5 - C - *Huckleberry Finn*

Whose Birthday? (page 86)

Baboon - 11 years old
Raccoon - 6 years old
Lion - 8 years old
Duck - 4 years old
Turtle - 8 years old
Elephant - 4 years old

Baboon is the oldest, but it is Turtle's birthday.

Wheel Fun (page 88)

Brian in car 9 will be the last one off.

Think Again (page 89)

1. You have two.
2. Eight
3. 24
4. One. Then it won't be empty.
5. Halfway. After that, she's running out again.
6. There is no dirt in a hole.
7. 1 hour. You'd take it at 12:00, 12:30, and 1:00.
8. A nickel and the other one would be a quarter.
9. NINE
10. Both weigh a pound.
11. 3

Locker Up! (pages 90-91)

Max - 37, 5 ,7
Millie- 11, 6, 17
Dotty - 35, 8, 11
Roy - 4, 27, 8
Lee - 10, 9, 7

The Audition Decision (page 93)

Macbeth - Roy, Snowman - Millie, Scarecrow - Lee, Tree - Max

Ref-a-Reason (page 93)

The Jets lost 50 yards and went back to the end zone.

Number Encumber (page 95)

What kind of numbers never stay in one place? ROAMIN' NUMERALS

Classroom Chaos (page 97)

What does the king use to get his drawbridge to work?
THE KING USES REMOAT CONTROL.

On the Ropes (page 98)

1-Lee, 2-Max, 3-Millie, 4-Rita, 5-Roy, 6-Brian, 7-Dotty

Cash-a-teria (page 100)

Linc - $2.55, Millie - $2.19, Max - $3.08, Roy - $1.89, Rita - $3.00
Max spent the most, Roy spent the least, and Rita spent exactly $3.00.

Report Odds (page 101)

Reading - Writing - Geography
Gym - Music - Art - Shop - Health - Library
History - Penmanship - Mathematics - Science - Spanish

Play Ball (page 102)

1. B-shortstop
2. A-single
3. A-fly ball
4. C-innings
5. B-pitcher
6. B-shutout
7. C-strikes
8. C-World Series
9. B-home run
10. C-umpire
11. B-ball

Opus Focus (page 103)

kazoo, saxophone, harmonica, piano, tubas, oboe, cornet, piccolo

Happyzippupz (page 103)

1. Clover
2. Go signal
3. Grass
4. Dollar bill
5. Frogs
6. Honeydew melon
7. Evergreen trees
8. Lime
9. Olives
10. Lettuce
11. Grapes
12. Martians
13. Greenland
14. Slime
15. Envy

Band in Boston (page 104)

A-wrong mouthpiece
B-no keyboard
C-no pedals
D-wrong mouthpiece
E-slide and bell are too far apart
F-no plug
G-no bellows
H-no electrical cord
I-guitar doesn't need a bow
J-not so many tuning keys
K-wrong mouthpiece
L-wrong mouthpiece
M-whistle and harmonica mix

A Puzzle of Note (page 105)

Letter Lines (page 106)

WHAT DO THEY CALL ALASKAN COWS? ESKIMOOS

The Big Pictures (page 107)

1. Soda can
2. Music bow
3. Playing card
4. Golf club
5. Can opener
6. Pepper shaker
7. Hard hat
8. Banana
9. Rubber bands
10. Fire extinguisher
11. Bicycle horn
12. Seashell

Crack the Code (page 108)

What is the center of gravity?
THE LETTER V.
Why would you put sugar on your pillow?
TO HAVE SWEET DREAMS.
Where can you always find happiness?
IN THE DICTIONARY.

Listing Links (page 109)

LEFT- hand - rail - way - side - walk - in - step - father - figure - head - cold - cream - puff - ball - game - show - off - BEAT

Smaller Words (page 109)

Red

Lists (page 109)

A-16 B-4 C-14

A Horse of a Different Color (page 111)

C

Too Much Turkey! (page 112)

A-1 B-4 C-7 D-3 E-5 F-6 G-2

Dotty (page 113)

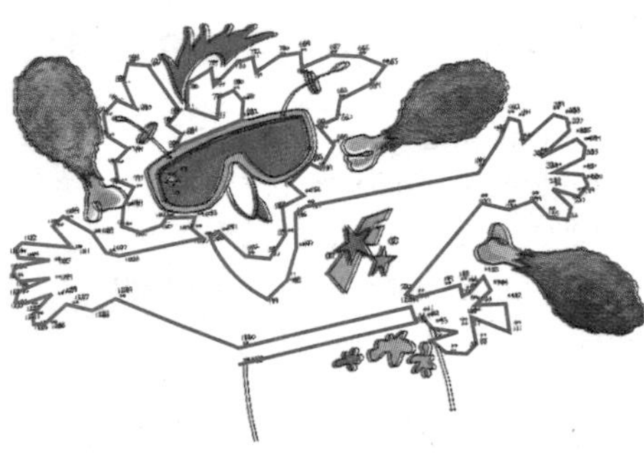

Something I Ate . . . (page 114)

1. Late
2. Date
3. Gate
4. State
5. Plate
6. Grate
7. Pirate
8. Karate
9. Celebrate
10. Approximate

Nature Hike (page 115)

SHRUBS
CAMPSITE
NEST
FOX
PATHWAY
TWIGS
ROCK
LIZARD
QUAIL
SKY
BERRIES
LAKE
OWL
RIVER
LEAF
STREAM
GRASS
BIRD
TREES
MOSS
MOOSE
WILLOW
NATURE
CLIFFS
BLUEJAY
TRACKS

October Items (page 117)

#2 and #6 are incorrect.

The Huddle Befuddle (page 119)

B shows the play called.

Mystery Want Ads (page 120)

1. Hey Diddle Diddle
2. Little Bo Peep
3. Peter Rabbit
4. Cinderella
5. Little Red Riding Hood
6. London Bridge Is Falling Down
7. Three Little Pigs
8. Old Woman Who Lived in a Shoe
9. Queen of Hearts
10. Wee Willie Winkie

What Does That Mean? (page 121)

1. Man overboard
2. Onion rings
3. A friend in need
4. Scattered drizzles
5. What goes up must come down
6. Half time
7. Feeling under the weather
8. Be with you in a minute
9. Reptiles

New World Search (page 122)

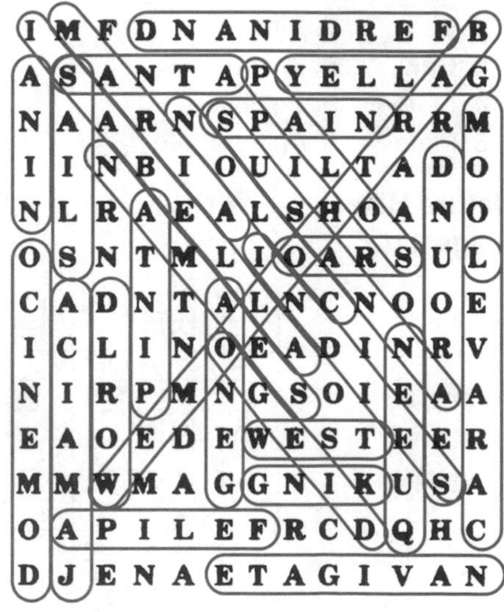

The name of one of Columbus's patrons was Friar Antonio de Marchena

Snow Row Row (page 124)

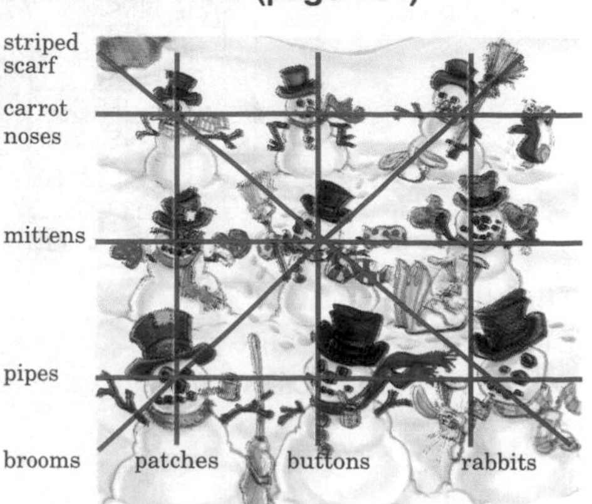
striped scarf
carrot noses
mittens
pipes
brooms
patches
buttons
rabbits

Snow Code (page 125)

DID ANYONE LAUGH WHEN
YOU FELL?
NO, BUT THE ICE MADE
A FEW CRACKS.

Money Matters I (page 126)

Dad - Orange car
Dan - Karate Cows game
Rae - Bug farm

Money Matters II (page 126)

$18.86

Holiday Shopping (page 127)

Present for Tiny Tim.
Pick up Dad's new suit.
Get candy for the table.
We need decorations for the house.
Buy Dad a new hammer.
Don't forget the turkey!
Choose a hot pumpkin pie.
Bring Mom fresh flowers.

Tree Trimmings (page 127)

3

Dot Connection (page 128)

Light Logic (page 128)

Five

Some Things Never Change (page 129)

scarf, dial, pine cone, bucket

Holiday Wrap Up (page 132)

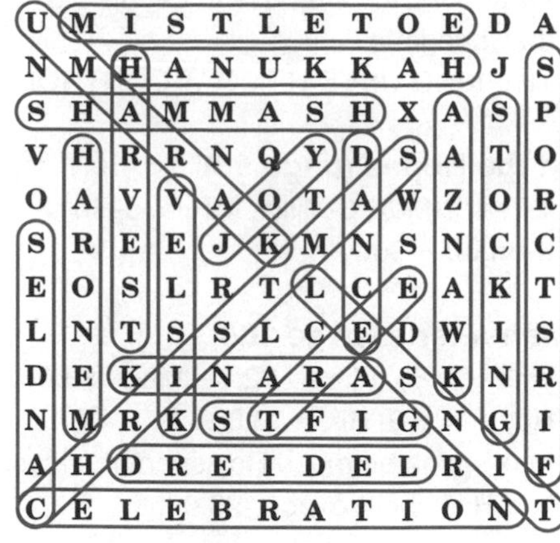

Shovel Trouble (page 133)

Farm Fun (page 135)

What do the cows say?
HAPPY MOO YEAR!

Echo Match (page 136)

Toe (foot) - Tow (truck)
Bowl (cereal) - Bowl (game)
Bow (and arrow) - Bow for a package
Fan (team) - Fan (cooling)
Chicken (bird) - chicken (afraid)
Coat (of paint) - Coat (on hanger)

Christmas Crossword (page 137)